You Wan⁻

MW01204151

A FAIRY TALE

Once upon a time, in a small village, there lived a poor old woman who loved to paint. Even though she had very little money, she gave her paintings away to anyone who asked for them. Sometimes they would give her a little money. Sometimes they would offer her vegetables or fruit. She was always very grateful for anything they gave her.

One day as she was walking in the woods, she spied a piece of old weathered board. She carried it home. This will be my next canvas she thought.

That night, in her dreams, she had a vision of the most beautiful place she had ever seen. She awoke and thought, "I must paint it right away before I forget it."

So she took the old weathered board and positioned it on her easel. The old woman painted feverishly, afraid the peaceful scene would fade from her memory before she was finished.

When the painting was finished, she placed it under a canopy in the front yard where everyone who passed by could see it.

All who beheld the painting marveled at the beauty of the scene. "Where is this enchanting place?" they would ask. "We want to go there."

She would reply, "I only know of it in my dreams."

The fame of the beautiful painting spread and one day the king and queen of the small province came to see the painting.

"We have heard of a picture you have painted and we would like to see it. If it is as beautiful as everyone says it is we would like to purchase it. We will make you a handsome offer," the king said smiling.

The woman was so taken aback at the honor that she was speechless. But she gained her composure, bowed and took them over to the canopy where the picture had been covered with a cloth to protect it. When the king and queen saw the painting, the queen gasped, "I must have that painting and you must tell me where this place is. I want to build a castle there."

"I don't know where the place is. Everyone asks me but I can only say I saw it in my dreams."

The queen offered everything she could think of, short of her husband or the throne, but the woman held firm. She told them in a most respectful tone that she felt it belonged to the people and if it were in the castle not everyone would be able to see it. The queen could not argue that point.

As the fame of the painting spread, a very rich man came up to her cottage one day and demanded to see it. The little woman took him out to the canopy. As she threw back the cover, his squinty eyes opened wide and his hard gaze softened. He came up closer to the painting. He stared at it for a long time without saying a word.

"Where is this place? I want to go there."

"The old woman replied, as she had many times before. " I don't know, I only saw it in my dreams."

"Then sell me the painting, I can pay you anything you want. I have much wealth."

"Sir, she began, "I cannot sell it, it belongs to the people."

He tried to change her mind but could not. The rich man finally decided to move close enough to the village so he could come and see it every day.

One day a woman came up to the painting. She was pushing her daughter in a wheelchair.

"My daughter has been very ill but she heard about your painting of a beautiful land. She wanted so much to see it."

The child looked intently at the scene, staring at it for a long time.

Finally she turned to her mother and said, "I know where that place is."

"You do?" asked her mother surprised. No one else had any idea where it could be because there was not such a beautiful place on all the earth.

The little old lady smiled. "Where did my dream come from?" she asked.

The mother had a sad look on her face. She knew her daughter had very little time to live.

"Oh mother," the child exclaimed, "don't be sad. Don't you see? I'll soon be going there. She's painted my new home, she's painted heaven!"

A PARABLE

There once was a peaceful planet where everything was perfect. It was blanketed with beautiful billowy white clouds. This world had two suns to shine on the people and they were at just the right distance to warm it so that the planet was profuse with the loveliest of flowers and vegetation. At the right time, the clouds would give up their moisture and release just the right amount of rain. All the people thought pure thoughts-no doubts ever entered their minds and everybody helped each other.

One day though, a dark cloud appeared on the planet. The people looked up at the sky and noticed it. It put doubts in their minds and soon they were arguing among themselves. When they did, the cloud got bigger and split into smaller clouds. It happened so fast that it caught the white clouds unaware. They called a council because the people were beginning to fight and even killing each other. What should they do? The dark clouds hurled lightning bolts and drenched the planet with floods so that some people were drowned.

"What are we going to do?" they ask each other. Nothing like this had ever happened before. Finally, one of the elder clouds replied. "Remember how it used to be? Our home in space was an Eden, no one fought, everyone worked together and everyone loved each other. What changed that?"

"That black cloud," they all exclaimed in unison.

"And what did he bring?" the elder cloud asked.' They thought for a moment. Bad thoughts, fear, distrust, hate, they all related the negatives this one cloud had introduced into their perfect world.

"And that's when our world and our people began to suffer, right?"

"Right." They all agreed with one voice.

"So we have to have faith that we can turn things back to the way they were before this cloud came to our world otherwise there will be no hope for our people." They all agreed. "So let's get started."

The smaller white clouds went down to the people in forms of mist and whispered thoughts of faith and hope and filled their hearts with the love they had before the black cloud came. The elder white clouds in the heavens surrounded all the dark clouds and encircled them with a girdle of love. The dark clouds were completely absorbed by the love of the white clouds until there was nothing left but the beautiful pure white clouds that had originally circled the planet.

Once again, their Eden was restored and peace and love filled all the people.
1 Corinthians 13:13 And now these three remain: faith, hope and love, but the greatest of these is love.

BEWARE OF E-MAIL

I picked up the photo and forced myself to look at it. Then I tore it into little pieces and threw it in the trash. I shuddered to think how close I had come to ruining and maybe even losing my life. I wanted to forget that entire part of my life but I knew I would always carry the scar.

I was born into a comfortable family life and really wanted for nothing. My mom and dad were very devoted to each other and did almost everything together. I was an only child so, of course, there was no sibling rivalry.

All went well until dad died unexpectedly. Mom couldn't seem to cope without dad. She was totally devastated. She developed almost every phobia imaginable, claustrophobia, agoraphobia, xenophobia, you name it, she had it. My mom became a total invalid. I tried to be a good daughter and take care of her. I was just out of high school but put off going to college so I could stay with her and try to get her out of her depression. The doctor had put her on so much medication that she slept most of the time. I prepared the meals, cleaned the house and tried to put on a cheerful face for mom, but it wasn't easy. If it had not been for my very close friend, Sarah, I'm afraid I would have wound up in the hospital or mental ward.

Even with all the medication to calm her down and the help of a psychiatrist, my mom passed away one year later on the same day my dad had died. I think she had harbored that date in her mind the entire year of her life.

I hated to see her die. I felt bad that I was not important enough in her life to fill the void that dad had left. But, in a way, I knew they were both together now and that she was at peace. In that way, I was relieved.

But now I found myself alone in my parent's big house. In my grief I turned to my friend, Sarah. She was different from me- very vivacious with her petite frame and long raven hair. She was a beauty.

I, on the other hand, was a plain Jane with thin straight hair the color of a mouse, cut short and plastered close to my face. I was a couple of inches taller but more than a few pounds heavier. She was always the one with the boyfriends and I was always the one who stayed home and watched TV. But even with all her boyfriends, she had never found one good enough to marry.

I was glad and it never dawned on me to be jealous of her beauty because now I really needed someone to talk to and I was grateful for her unwavering friendship.

After mom died, she was over more often. One day, while I was reading my e-mail on the computer, Sarah suggested I e-mail a certain religious man with whom she had become acquainted through the internet. His name was Ryan Varner. He was the leader of a progressive religious movement in California.

Now I know what you're thinking. How could I be so naïve to e-mail someone I don't know? But I really thought Sarah was level headed and would never do anything without first checking out the individual. It's not like I'm meeting him and Sarah has been corresponding with him for some time. So I took the plunge, so to speak. My first e-mail was a one of introduction. I stated I was a friend of Sarah's. To my surprise, I received an e-mail back immediately. He told me how grateful he was to Sarah for bringing me to his ministry of love and that he was sure I would be rewarded abundantly. I don't why, but that made me feel very important.

Now don't get me wrong, I was happy for Sarah's friendship but at this point in my life I really craved a male figure. Looking back on it now I realize how vulnerable I was.

Sarah and I e-mailed him quite frequently over the next few months. We even sent money to him. We always addressed him as Pastor Ryan instead of Pastor Varner. He said he felt closer to his flock when they addressed him by his first name. He called his place of worship a tabernacle. He had many different ideas but I thought, that's what makes him progressive. In fact, the next few months I was completely mesmerized by him. It seemed to me he had combined eastern culture with western religion. To some people, I'm sure, he would have seemed a visionary, a dreamer, idealistic but I was completely taken in by his ideas.

Pastor Ryan invited us to come out and visit his tabernacle. He was hoping we might be able to help him start a movement in our area. He had an assistant who could come back with us and help get us started.

Sarah was excited about the prospect of meeting Pastor Ryan, which she sometimes addressed as just Ryan. I wondered if maybe she might not be getting too serious about their relationship but I said nothing. He had sent us a photo of himself and I had to admit he looked rather handsome. Probably in his late twenties or early thirties he seemed a bit old for both of us. However he had never mentioned having been married. I decided if she wanted him, I wouldn't stand a chance anyway.

We planned for the trip; actually, Sarah planned for the trip. I had never flown and was apprehensive. Did I mention I have acrophobia?

The flight to L. A. was easier than I thought. We had seats in the center aisle so I could only see an occasional cloud.

Pastor Ryan said he would meet us in the airport terminal and that he would be wearing a white suit. We told him we would also be wearing white.

Now Los Angeles airport is a large place but it was not crowded. Sarah spotted him almost immediately. She started to wave to him.

"Why is he wearing a turban?" I asked.

"I don't know." she replied lowering her arm.

Just as we were walking toward Ryan, the police rushed toward him and handcuffed him.

We could only stand aghast. Sarah found her voice first.

"What are you doing?" she demanded.

"Lady," one of the officers responded, "we've been trying to round up this guy for a long time. He's been running an e-mail scam pretending he's the leader of a progressive religious movement. He tries to get people to send all their money to him. He says he has a tabernacle. There is no tabernacle, only a million-dollar home, a yacht and a Mercedes. Did you send him any money?"

We had to admit we did and knew at that moment we had been fleeced.

The officer looked at us and just shook his head. Ryan wouldn't look at us. We both felt so ashamed that we had believed his lies.

On the trip back we were both silent. We were still trying to understand how he could have deceived us so completely.

For weeks to come, we still felt violated but finally realized if we retreated into our shell that Ryan would have won.

So once again we decided to launch out, however, a little more cautiously. This time there will be no more eastern, western, turban, tabernacle, mumbo-jumbo through e-mails. We'll make sure we know what we're getting into even if we have to check it out with the Better Business Bureau.

BIG RED RIDING HOOD

They call me Big Red Riding Hood. I drive a souped-up Harley and have a grandma who's a hypochondriac. Oh, and there's a two-legged wolf by the name of Ralph that keeps following me. He seems to have the ridiculous idea that I find him irresistible. I don't know whether he likes bigger and stronger women but I easily outweigh him by fifty pounds and I'm half a head taller. I don't want to hurt the guy but he really irritates me.

Anyway, I like to look in on granny often to see how she is doing. The other day she called me and told me, in addition to all her other ailments, she was suffering from a really terrible cold and might not pull through. I decided I would take some homemade chicken noodle soup to her.

So I set out on my Harley for the five-mile trip to granny's house. She lived on the edge of a dense forest that also added to her hypochondria. I have tried to get her to move but I sometimes think she enjoys living there since she knows that it worries me.

As I drove up to the little cottage, I noticed the paper lying on the ground. I picked it up.

The front door was unlocked. As I opened it, my eyes had trouble adjusting from the bright light of the sun to the darkness of the room.

"Granny," I called out but got no answer.

I slowly made my way over to the window and pulled up the shade.

I looked over toward the bed and noticed her teeth in a glass on the nightstand.

"Granny," I called again.

I walked over to the bed. All I could see was a frilly nightcap sticking out from under the covers.

"Granny, are you ok?" I grabbed the covers and pulled them down to reveal two huge eyes peering out from under a pair of eyeglasses.

"Granny, what are you doing wearing your glasses in bed?"

"The better to see you with my dear," came a squeaky voice.

I pulled the bed covers down further. It was not granny in the bed, it was Ralph.

I grabbed him around the neck. "What have you done with my granny?"

Ralph got loose from my grip, jumped out of bed and ran out the door.

I started to run after him but thought I had better find granny first. I ran through the house. "Granny, granny, where are you? Are you OK?"

Finally I heard a muffled sound coming from the bathroom. She was crouching in the corner, her hands and feet tied and a gag in her mouth.

"What happened?" I asked, as I removed the gag and untied her.

"That crazy friend of yours tied me up and threw me in the bathroom. He was going to wait for you and try to fool you into thinking he was me."

"Granny, you should know by now that I can't stand Ralph. Are you OK?"

Granny nodded yes and after tucking her into bed I took off to locate Ralph.

I finally caught up with him, just as he was about to go up to his apartment

I parked my Harley and dismounted. When Ralph saw me coming, he started running but I ran after him and tackled him. After some animated conversation and a few well-aimed blows, Ralph got loose and hobbled up the steps and into the building. I decided to let Ralph go because I think he finally got the message. I don't think we'll be seeing much of Ralph anymore.

CURMUDGEON

My body wouldn't stop shaking even though my sister held me as tight as she could. I suddenly realized just how close I came to being killed. My curiosity had always been my problem and this time it was almost my undoing.

My sister Lucy was 19, three years older than me. We had each other and that was it. Five years ago our dad ran away with another woman and two years ago mom passed away so we were on our own. Our neighbors helped us when we needed help so it wasn't as if we had nobody to look after us but still there was a void caused by infidelity and death.

Lucy was the practical one and I guess I was the dreamer and daredevil. I was always looking for adventure and in the small town of Locust Grove there wasn't much to choose from. But all that changed one day when an elderly man moved in to the old Carson house on the hill. The house had been vacant for several years and not kept up very well. We watched as the van unloaded his furniture which consisted of a single bed, a table and two chairs and several huge crates.

I thought I would give him a couple of days to settle in and then welcome him in to the neighborhood by taking him some cookies. And at his age he might have led a very interesting life.

As I walked up the hill I tried to rehearse what to say to him. "Hi, my name is Sarah Hudson. I want to welcome you into the neighborhood. I baked you some cookies." I knocked on the door and yelled out. "HELLO." I heard the shuffling of feet and the sound of a cane tapping on the floor. Through the screen door I could a figure coming toward me. "Whatda ya want?" He scowled.

I was taken aback by this unexpected behavior. He did not open the door but I could see he had exceptionally harsh features-like he had seen rough times. His face was gaunt and he looked sickly. I think at one time he might have been close to six feet tall but now he was bent over and leaning on his cane.

"I-I-I just wanted to welcome you to our little town. I didn't mean to bother you." I stuttered.

"Well you did, so go away."

"Won't you take the cookies?" I pleaded. "I baked them just for you."

"Leave 'em on the porch." He motioned to the floor. "Now go away and don't come back"

Well my ego was definitely deflated but I was more determined than ever to make him my friend. There was finally something exciting to do in Locust Grove.

My sister was not in favor of my pursuing his friendship any further.

"You don't know anything about him. He could be hiding from the police, he could be an ax murderer, he could be anything."

That's my sister I thought, always thinking the worst about people.

In the next few months I continued to visit him. He finally told me his name, Adolph Maas, although I had no way of knowing if that was his real name. He said he had been in the army but refused to say any more than that.

He never invited me into his house; we always sat on the front porch and I always had to initiate the conversation. It was painful but I was determined to make this man my friend if it took me the rest of my life.

I told my sister that I was not making much headway but at least I knew his name and that he was in the army

"You be careful," she cautioned. "You still don't know anything about him for sure."

One day I went up and knocked on the door as usual but he did not come to the door. I tugged on the screen door. It was unlatched. I called, "Mr. Maas." No answer. I couldn't resist. I opened the door and walked in. The table and chairs sat in the middle of the room. A lamp sat on the table. I went over to inspect the lampshade which was nothing like I had ever seen before. I felt it and quickly drew my hand away. It felt like rawhide. Why would he have a lampshade of rawhide? Then a horrible thought hit me. The army he was in was not the United States Army but rather the German Army. He was actually an SS officer and the lampshade was actually the skin of one of his victims. The realization sent chills down my spine.

Suddenly I heard footsteps coming closer. I turned to see Adolph Maas facing me.

"I told you never to come in this house." He hissed. "You have put both of us in a dangerous predicament. I can't let you go. You know too much."

"Look." I pleaded, "I won't tell. I know it happened a long time ago. They probably don't even care about it anymore."

"You're wrong, that was the reason I came to this town, to hide and you had to stick your nose in everything and I can't let you tell anyone where I am."

"What are you going to do? I promise I won't tell."

"I can't take that chance," he said as he tried to grab my arm.

I ran for the door, but he blocked my way. I scrambled over to the table and picked up the lamp and threw it at him. It caught him off guard and knocked him to the floor. But he was still between me and the door. I tried to run around him to get to the door, but he caught my ankle and dragged me down. We scuffled on the floor. I knew this was a fight for my life, he knew I would tell if I broke free. He was beating me mercilessly on the head with his cane, and I was losing consciousness fast. Just as I thought my time had come, the door flew open and the police arrived with my sister. She helped me up. I was shaking so hard, I thought I would fall apart.

Finally, after I gained my strength and stopped shaking, Lucy told me she had given the police the name Adolph Maas. He had actually felt safe enough to use his real name. They found he was wanted for crimes he had committed against the Jews during the Second World War.

Well, things have settled down here, the Carson's house is vacant again. Can't wait to see who moves in next.

DO YOU KNOW WHO KILLED DOROTHY MILLER?
I DO. IT WAS....

Dorothy was married to a millionaire.
Of course she loved Her husband very much.
Yes, she was a very dEvoted wife.
Of course, they had little pRoblems like all couples.
Unfortunately sometimes they are blown out of proportion.
Kyle, her Husband, saw no problem.
Now Dorothy was not what you would call a raving beauty.
Oh I don't mean she was Ugly but Kyle could sure have done better.
Why he picked Dorothy over all the other women that had flocked around him was a myStery.
When he announced his plans to marry her, his parents were aghast.
How, out of all the women he could have had, would he choose Dorothy Carter?
Oh her parents were not poor but they certainly weren't like the Millers.
Kyle's parents owned the Miller Manufacturing Company.
It was a company established By his grandparents and would always be in the family.
Leland Miller, his grAndfather, had come from England in the early 1900's.
Leland started out small, making beautiful furNiture by hand but now it had grown into a huge business.
Ethan Allen recognizeD him as an equal.

Dorothy's pArents thought the world of Kyle and felt lucky to have him as part of their family.
Dorothy felt all her thoughts aNd dreams had come true.
On occasion Dorothy woulD practice writing her last name Miller in different waYs like a school girl.
Riches really did not mean that much to Dorothy, she just loved KYle.
On one occasion, as she was visiting with her best friend, YyVonne.
The subject of Kyle came up and Dorothy was all too happy to talk about her husband.
Her friend, Yyvonne mentioned that she had seen Kyle Out with some striking beauty.
"YyvoNne," Dorothy hissed, "how dare you say that about Kyle.
My husbaNd would never be unfaithful to me.
I never want to sEe you again.
Leave my husband and me alone.
Listen to me Yyvonne, I mean what I say."
Every muscle in Dorothy's body ached.
Really, she did not like confrontations.
It was inconceivable that Kyle was having an affair.
Dorothy trusted Kyle completely.
On the day Dorothy was killed.
It was a cold, cloudy December morning.
The body of Dorothy Miller had been stabbed multiple times.
Why would anyone want to kill Dorothy?
An innocent person who never wanted to hurt anyone?

[This is an acrostic as well as a mystery puzzle. Solve the puzzle by looking through the text and finding the capital letters in the sentences where they should not be.]

ELECTRONIC MADAGASCAR HISSING COCKROACHES

I now call the newly formed union of the Six-Million Dollar Madagascar Hissing Cockroaches and Roachettes to order. As some of you may or may not know humans have finally flipped their gourd so to speak and have armed us with amazing electronic gadgets. They are outfitting each one of us with a handy dandy backpack outfitted with a circuit board that has a microcontroller wireless signal receiver and a lithium-ion polymer battery just so we can locate where these humans are.

Did we have any trouble before? I don't recall any complaints. You ask why they did this. What was their motive? You have to realize that when dealing with a sub-intelligent species such as humans it's difficult to bring yourself down to their level of thinking but we will definitely take full advantage of their stupidity.

I have asked our head seamstress, Sophia to outfit each of us with a shirt that has a blue and white logo. It will have the letters SR for Super Roaches embroidered on the front. To make ourselves even more intimidating we will wear red cloaks on our backs. Roaches will wear red shorts and roachettes will wear red skirts. When they see us coming in all our glory it will probably give them a heart attack. And the further irony is the fact that they made it all possible for us.

I am asking Commander Crochesster to arm each one of you with a dagger which Bernard our blacksmith will forge in his shop. It will be attached to your shorts or skirt for protection.

As you go into battle I will be on the side lines since they have equipped me with a camera and will be filming your fights for future review. These pictures will go into our archives for generations to come. Also after each battle Commander Crochesster will go over the maneuvers to see how we can improve. This is an exciting time for us. Soon the entire earth will be ours and humans will be our slaves.

All eligible roaches and roachettes will be required to enlist in our army with the exception of the members of the Roachette Hissing Glee Club. We do need some entertainment and I love the way they hiss "You Light Up My Life." Also this will include members of the orchestra. I have heard they are working on an exciting version of Rimsky-Korsakov's Flight of the Bumblebee.

Even though humans have provided us with all this armor we must not become too cocky. There is little time to lose. They are not too bright but it may eventually dawn on them that what they did could have been a mistake.

We need to delegate certain tasks to our most capable citizens therefore I will form different committees to fulfill these needs. I have already assigned the Department of Entertainment to Rachel Roachette. The head of the Department of Defense of course is Commander Crochesster. I am creating a Department of the Military and Harry I am naming you as its head. I have seen how your little roaches and roachettes stand at attention when you address them and I am certain I can count on you to make sure the humans that we take captive are kept busy producing food for us.

You must pardon my exuberance. We have been on this earth millions of years but with everything the humans have done for us we will rule the world. We will be invincible. We will never die.

"FINALS"

I can't believe this is happening to me. There's not much time left. How did I get into this mess? My folks always made me go to church and Sunday school. Never bought me a fancy car like Roger had. Told me I should be satisfied with what I had. Well, I wasn't. And if they wouldn't buy it for me, well I would just have to take it. Didn't buy into that Hell and Damnation stuff anyway. I figure you just live for today. Got my fancy car but wound up killin' a family doin' it. Judge didn't like me. Sentenced me to death. Even appeals didn't help. Just finished my last meal-shrimp, French fries and chocolate sundae. Got butterflies in my stomach, could hardly swallow. They ask me if I wanted a preacher, I said no. Maybe that was a mistake. Too late now. Here comes the Warden. I hear there are thirteen steps to the chair, I'm not gonna count 'em. My legs feel shaky. I know that stuff they preach in church is just a bunch of mumbo-jumbo and yet maybe I should have talked with that preacher. Too late now.

FULL MOON AND YOU

I had to go back. It had been seven months since Sarah had disappeared. It happened during the full moon on Halloween. That night she was so excited. I knew she had a date with him. She said, "I have something exciting to tell you but you have to wait until I come back."

She never came back.

Sarah lived with us. Her parents died in an automobile accident when she was eleven. That was ten years ago. I was seven years older and felt more like a mother to her. She grew to be a beautiful, tall blonde with a model-thin figure who dated all the studs in school. I on the other hand inherited my dad's figure, short and stocky with straight sun-streaked hair. It gave me little comfort to know that I was a little smarter than she was.

Sarah could have had any one she wanted but the day Sebastian came to town was the day she made up her mind he was the one. All dressed in black he gave me a feeling of uneasiness. It was as though he was hiding something. I think this is what attracted Sarah to him. He seemed attracted to her too. I felt like he was using her and I felt he knew what I was thinking. Mom did not approve of him either and was very upset that Sarah even associated with him. She tried her best to stop them from seeing each other, but her efforts were to no avail. Sarah would simply not listen to reason. I often heard the two arguing late into the night. To my mother the very thought of Sebastian and Sarah together was revolting. I tried to reason with her too.

"Why does he always dress in black?" I asked Sarah.

"He looks good in black," she replied in a haughty manner.

"Are you sure he's not in a satanic cult? He looks creepy."

"You're just so jealous," she screamed back at me. "He's very kind and gentle."

Anyway I knew in my heart that her date that night was with Sebastian and I was sure he was going to give her a ring.

I waited for her to come home. I wanted to apologize for what I had said but she didn't come home.

The next morning we reported her missing and voiced our concerns about Sebastian. The police went to the sports goods store where he worked. He seemed as disturbed as we were. He said he had waited in the park for her to come but she didn't show.

I had to return to work but while I was away I called mom every week to see if the police had been investigating Sarah's disappearance and if they found out anything but she said they would tell her nothing. I asked her about Sebastian and she told me he was still working at the sports goods store.

It only took me a couple of hours to get home and when I arrived I stopped at the house to say "Hi" to mom and then headed over to the police department. I was introduced to Captain Crowder who informed me it was an ongoing investigation and he couldn't tell me anything or he would be compromising the investigation.

"Well, can't you tell me if you have questioned Sebastian more thoroughly?"

"No."

"Can you tell me if he's a suspect?"

"No."

"Did you give him a lie detector test and did he pass it?"

"No, I told you it's an ongoing investigation and I can't tell you anything that might compromise the investigation."

"Well, I guess I will just have to question him myself."

"You stay away from him, he's bad news."

"Then you do suspect him."

"I didn't say that. I just don't want to have to fish your body out of the river."

"Well, it's been seven months and you haven't found Sarah's body yet." I called back as I stormed out the door. Why did I say Sarah's body? I don't know that she's dead. He just had me so upset.

I was fairly calm by the time I arrived at the sports goods store. There I found a completely different Sebastian. No longer was he dressed in black but in a powder blue shirt and gray slacks. He seemed shocked to see me but came over.

"I know you think I had something to do with Sarah's disappearance but please believe me, I didn't. I was going to give her a ring that night but she never showed up. I waited for three hours and then went home."

"Could we talk?" I asked.

"Sure, I get off in a few minutes. I'll meet you across the street at the café."

As I walked across the street I wasn't sure he really would come over or whether he was just saying that to make me feel that he was really sincere.

I watched as he left the store. He hesitated but then headed over to the café. He again stated that he had stayed three hours waiting for Sarah but that she never came and that he really did love her and wanted to marry her.

"Did you take a lie detector test?" I asked.

"Yes," he replied, "and I passed it. "Look, I want to find her as much as you do but I don't know where to start."

"Do you think the police are really investigating her disappearance?" I asked.

"They say they are and that's why they won't tell us anything- ongoing investigation you know and they might release something that only the guilty party knows."

"I know. I talked to a Captain Crowder"

"Grouchy, isn't he?"

"Yes, he's quite a challenge."

Sebastian and I talked for a few minutes more and then I drove home. It was still light and I strolled around in the yard before I went in to the house. Mom was at the table reading the paper.

"Mom, when did you plant that rose garden in the back yard? You told me you don't even like roses."

HOW ICE CREAM HAS AFFECTED MY LIFE

My memories of ice cream are bittersweet. I both met and lost my first, second and third husbands because of this scrumptious dish. I met my first husband at the local ice cream parlor. We were in separate booths. He was engaged in devouring a banana split. I had settled for a double scoop of Tutti Fruitti. He smiled at me and invited me over to his booth. I know what you're thinking. You're thinking I should have said no because you can't be too careful these days, although that was over twenty years ago. But he had such a handsome and honest face and that was before Ted Bundy, Jeffrey Dahmer and Charles Manson so I took my Tutti Fruitti and went over to his booth. As we talked I realized we had much in common-we both were crazy about ice cream. In fact, while we were enjoying our ice cream, we made a game out of going through the alphabet and naming all the different flavors we could with each letter.

Each day we met at the ice cream parlor and three months later we were married. Of course, we spent our honeymoon at the ice cream capitol of the world, Le Mars, Iowa. You can't imagine how many flavors we sampled-it was sheer heaven.

After we were married we made it a habit to eat ice cream twice a day. We fixed shakes, banana splits; we even created our own concoctions like a huge ice cream soda in one of our tall flower vases. In fact, it was so big that we had to put it on the floor and use bamboo straws to reach the bottom.

Then, one day while Roger was watching TV and enjoying a fruit and nut ice cream, he started choking. He managed to get up out of the chair and I ran over to him. I tried to do the Heimlich maneuver which I had seen many times but all the ice cream he had been eating had gone to his waist and when I tried to get my arms around him I lost my balance and we both fell to the floor. He was now starting to turn blue and I was panicking. I tried to do artificial respiration on him. Now I want you to know I had taken a life saving course and had done artificial respiration on a dummy. Unfortunately, I was told if my patient had been real he would have died. That's the main reason I did not become a nurse. Finally it occurred to me to call 911. By now Roger was turning three shades of blue, light, medium and dark.

By the time the Medics arrived Roger was only one shade of blue-dark. They were too late. He could not be revived.

I mourned for him. Even though we had not known each other very long, we had shared gallons of ice cream together. I could not bring myself to go back to the little ice cream parlor where first we met because there were too many sad memories there.

My friend, Roberta, finally talked me into going with her to a new restaurant that had just opened in the mall. I wasn't really hungry so I only ordered a sandwich and tea. Roberta suggested I try a dessert. She said I should try a piece of apple pie with just a small scoop of ice cream. Would I be able to handle the ice cream or would it trigger too many sad memories? When it came it looked SO appetizing. But as I started to eat it, tears started running down my cheeks. The owner of the restaurant happened to see me and noticed how upset I was and came over to our table.

"Is everything all right?" he asked concerned.

I couldn't talk but Roberta explained that I had just lost my husband while eating ice cream. He was very sympathetic and showed it by not only tearing up the bill but by inviting me out on a date. It so happens that his wife had recently passed away.

Two months later Rodney and I were married. I found out he also enjoyed ice cream. I suggested we build an addition on to the restaurant and have it exclusively for ice cream. At first we did very well with the new addition but as the new wore off so did the sales. Rodney started having problems keeping the restaurant afloat and he became more aloof. One day he just jumped off the bridge. Now if there had been water below and if he'd changed his mind as he went down, he might have survived but there wasn't. I could only assume he meant to commit suicide. Once again I found myself a widow.

By now I was beginning to wonder if there was something wrong with me or whether my love for ice cream was my albatross. I decided I would seek the advice of a psychiatrist. Horace, my psychiatrist, assured me it was all in my head, it was just my imagination. He even said he would be willing to work with me after hours. I thought that was very sweet of him and we became close friends, in fact, we were married three months later. I found out that Horace had quite a sweet tooth. He was especially partial to homemade ice cream so we bought an ice cream freezer and made ice cream every night after dinner. We even invited some of his patients over and held meetings at the house.

This went well until one evening during the meeting and just before we were ready to eat our homemade ice cream which I was going to top with homegrown strawberries and whipped cream, one of the patients pulled out a gun and shot Horace. Everyone was horrified. I didn't realize his patients were so troubled. I was in the kitchen. His back was to me. I quickly grabbed the iron skillet that was drying on the stove and sneaked up behind him before he was able to shoot anyone else. With all my force I brought the skillet down on his head. I ran over to Horace but it was too late. I could not detect a pulse. I called the police and by the time they arrived the patient had regained consciousness. They took him away to jail where they later committed him to an asylum.

Well, I am a widow again but I'm not about to give up ice cream. I think it's the men that are the problem.

I had almost finished writing my fictional story about ice cream and mentioned to my daughter that I couldn't remember anything notable to write about ice cream so I had to think up a story.

She informed me that she remembered lots of things when she was growing up-like the Rocky Road we used to get that had 5 scoops of different flavors on it.

That triggered my memory and I started remembering the delicious banana splits we used to enjoy after church on Sunday. They were so big that you had to have a paper under them because the marshmallow crème would spill over the sides and the nuts would fall down on the paper. One person couldn't eat all of it so we shared.

I also remembered making snow ice cream when we lived on the farm. We gathered the snow and added the milk, sugar and vanilla. It left a little to be desired but it was cold. Later in life I made snow ice cream by making a thin pudding and adding the amount of snow you wanted. It tasted just like homemade ice cream. This triggered another memory. In the summer, when we lived on the farm we made homemade ice cream every Saturday night in our hand cranked ice cream maker. We took turns cranking and when it got too hard to crank we knew it was ready to eat. I always felt it was almost sacrilegious to put fruit on top of homemade ice cream so I never did.

I remember one time when I made snow ice cream my grandson Andy ate it too fast and wound up with a terrific headache. We had forgotten to warn him that commercial ice cream had quite a bit of air incorporated into it but snow ice cream had none.

I'm glad Debbie jogged my memory. It brought back many pleasant memories.

I GOT ON THE TRAIN

I walked back to the apartment with a heavy heart. I had just buried my best friend. We had been roommates for four years. We met in college and became soul mates. Our interests were almost identical-both wanted to become astronomers. Ann Marie was so much better at math than I was. If she had not nurtured me through calculus I would not have graduated. Now just as we were ready for the real world she was gone- taken by cancer at the age of twenty-five. It had come like a thief in the night. There was no warning and her life was snuffed out in less than a month. I was not ready for this. I didn't see how I could go on without her.

I walked on staring down at the brick sidewalk, my eyes filling with tears and not really seeing anything.

"I was told to give you this." I blinked trying to focus through my tears. A white haired man in a dark suit handed me an envelope. His skin was pale but his eyes were dark and penetrating. Before I could even respond he had disappeared.

I finished the walk in a daze. I had no idea what was happening. Did I just imagine the stranger? No, I had the envelope in my hand so that part was real and it was addressed to me.

When I reached my apartment, I opened the envelope. The letter was an invitation for a ride on a very special train. It was called the U-train. It further stated," you have been especially selected by our committee for this trip and will be picked up at your apartment at precisely 6:00am Tuesday May 2nd. Please be ready and bring letter."

May 2nd, that was tomorrow! If I took up their offer would I regret it or if I didn't would I regret it more? If Ann Marie were here she would say, "Go for it." So for her I'll do it.

The next morning, promptly at 6:00am the doorbell rang. It was the same man who had handed me the envelope the day before.

"Follow me." He ordered as he preceded me down the steps. He opened the back door of the limousine and motioned me to enter. He said nothing the rest of our trip which took us out past the city. There in a wooded area sat a most unusual train. It consisted of three identical cars. It had no engine or caboose and no train tracks were visible. He escorted me to a door where another man greeted me and helped me on to the train. I handed him the letter and turned to thank the man who had brought me to the train but he had already disappeared.

"Welcome to Catherine Allen," he seemed to be announcing my arrival to the passengers in the car. The man, also dressed in black and looking like a double for the man that brought me to the train, pointed me to my seat.

"We will be traveling much faster than the speed of light but you will feel no discomfort." the man continued.

"But," I corrected him, "Einstein proved that nothing can travel faster than the speed of light."

"With all due respect to your Mr. Einstein the Boss can do anything He wants to do."

"Who IS your boss?" I asked but he left without answering my question.

I settled back in my seat and then a voice came from nowhere.

"You are on the U Train. You will see the universe as no one has ever seen it before."

For some reason I felt no fear, no anxiety. I leaned back in my seat as we soared at impossible speeds. Bright lights, then darkness alternated as we sped through space.

The voice announced we were almost at the constellation Pleiades. I remembered when Ann Marie and I first saw them in the telescope. They were so beautiful and bright. They are also called the Seven Sisters. In mythology they were the seven daughters of the Titan Atlas and the nymph Pleione.

Suddenly our train entered into indescribable brilliance of swirling blues, reds and yellows. I closed my eyes for fear of being blinded. The voice continued, "We are nearing a planet similar to yours that circles the largest star you call Alcyone. On this planet are those who loved flowers during their lifetime. There is no night here and always the right amount of rain so the plants continue to thrive without much care." The train edged closer to the planet and we saw people tending their gardens and the most beautiful flowers I have ever seen.

From my astronomy class I recalled the Pleiades were approximately 430 light years away from earth. This can't be true. This cannot be happening to me. This has to be a dream.

But my train or dream kept speeding through the cosmos. Patterns of light and darkness assailed my eyes.

The voice once again spoke.

"We are heading toward the constellation Orion. All the stars that you can see with the naked eye from earth contain planets dedicated to the sciences. We will be enveloped by the red giant star Betelgeuse but our next stop will be the planet that revolves around Alnilam, the center star in Orion's belt.   It is 1300 light years from earth and dedicated to astronomy. Our latest recruit just arrived from earth and she wanted to study Cepheid Variables. She also asked that her friend be invited to ride the U-train."

Was he talking about me? Was Ann Marie actually on this planet? Was she still alive and on a planet in a constellation far, far away. I wanted to be able to see her and wave at her but the voice continued.

"We are now at the farthest part of our journey. If you look ahead you will see a very brilliant light. Even though it is millions of light years from us we can go no closer. This is where our Boss lives, where all the banquets and meetings are held. You will be at the end of your destination within minutes."

I was still in a daze as I got off the train. The same man who picked me up at my apartment took me back without saying a word.

Was it a dream? I was so confused. None of it made any sense. I lay down on the couch totally exhausted and fell asleep.

When I awoke my cosmic adventure was still on my mind. Suddenly I remembered I gave the man on the train my letter but I left the envelope on the table.

I hurried into the dining room. There on the table was the envelope with my name on it. It wasn't a dream after all.

I clutched the envelope and ran out into the night sky. Orion was up. I waved my envelope at the star Alnilam. Thanks Ann Marie, it was one heck of a train ride!

INNOCENCE LOST

The night air on the mountain was chilling as I gathered my ill-fitting coat around my frail body. On a moonless night the stars would be shining with a brilliance city people were not privy to and the Milky Way would weave its nebulous path across the sky. In the far distance I could barely see the lights of the city. But now there was no time to enjoy the celestial beauty. I was thankful for a gibbous moon to help light my way. Tonight I was running for my life.

My only hope of survival was to make it to the road which was about a quarter of a mile away and I dared not use my flashlight any more than I needed. The lights from the commune gave me little help. I knew that soon our shepherd's bodyguards would discover that I was not in my bed. They would come looking for me, the huge searchlights flooding the grounds. I made it to the hedge and breathed a sigh of relief. They had not missed me yet. The shrubbery beyond might give me enough cover to make it down to the road but I would still be on my own because the gate was always locked. Nothing but authorized vehicles was allowed to enter. If I made it to the gate perhaps I would have a chance. I stopped to catch my breath and started remembering how I got in the mess in which I now found myself.

I had always strived to be a positive person and looked at the glass half full but my parents decided that when I graduated from high school they had performed all their parental duties and that I was not welcome at home anymore. Where I was supposed to go they didn't say. I was just told to get a job and good luck.

However, I did have one friend who graduated with me. She allowed me to stay with her until I could find a job. This lasted a few weeks until she questioned my desire to actually look for employment so she decided that it was time for me to leave.

I finally found a job as an aid in a nursing home. It wasn't much, mostly cleaning up after patients and helping them with their food since I had no training but it gave me enough money to rent a small apartment in a poor neighborhood.

There I made friends with another girl my age. Sally seemed shy but eventually opened up to me. That's when she invited me to go to hear him; who Sally said was the most wonderful preacher in the world.

The first time I heard him he sounded a bit radical but very dynamic. His dream was to create a better world, one in which we would be free from its cares- a place far beyond the big city, high on a mountain. He would be our shepherd and we would be his sheep. Why did I not see the danger in that? But he was so charismatic, Sally was so nice and I had found people who loved me. There were about 100 of us and we pooled all our assets and although I had very little to give they made me feel welcome.

We found a bit of property high on a mountain far away from the city. Some of the men had been architects and builders on the outside and were handy with hammer and nails, so thanks to them we were soon able to put up the walls and later finish the inside as time permitted.

I must admit I was happy and felt comfortable. There were duties to do but everybody did their bit.

However as time went on our shepherd seemed more demanding, expecting sexual favors from some of the women.

Sally said he made unwelcome advances toward her. He also started to come to me and demand favors. I knew that he encouraged the husbands to go to their wives. Our shepherd said God expected us to create a large group of loyal people to bring his kingdom on earth. He also said he and Jesus were the only people that had a direct line to God. Of course our shepherd helped all he could by making himself available to any of the women at any time.

I approached Sally telling her I thought it was time to leave- that our shepherd was preaching something dangerous, but she seemed to be under his spell. As days went on, Sally seemed to actually throw herself at him. I tried to talk to her but she seemed so distant now. It's as if she tried to avoid me. Then I didn't see her for several days. Was she sick? Where was she? Why wouldn't they answer me? Why couldn't I see her? Without Sally, I felt lonely even though they were still friendly to me. No one would answer my question. That seemed very strange. One just doesn't disappear.

Things were changing fast. Our shepherd was becoming more radical and more suspicious of even his own flock. He spoke with more urgency and did not allow anyone to question his authority. He said with certainty his kingdom was coming soon and we must make ourselves ready to go to the next level. What did he mean by that? Suddenly a horrible thought entered my mind. Did our shepherd have in mind for us the same fate as the followers of Jim Jones, David Keresh and Heaven's Gate? I had to leave before it was too late and try to tell my story.

But the next day our shepherd had all the families gather together and prepare their evening meal. Then at the end of the day we would all go to our rooms. Our shepherd told us he would prepare a special elixir that would prepare us for our next level.

That was when I knew that the end was near and I had to try and escape.

I was almost at the gate now but how could I get over it? On the mountain I saw the searchlights come on. I knew they had found my room empty and were hunting for me. I was sure they would realize I was headed for the gate. His bodyguards started fanning out with their huge flashlights weaving back and forth. I had to get away from the gate because I would be an easy target. I looked for some cover, a bush or anything to hide under. But it was too late. I had already been spotted. As they came close I knew I would never have to drink our shepherd's elixir and I knew I would never be able to tell my story. As his bodyguard pulled the trigger darkness came over me.

"IT WAS A DARK AND STORMY NIGHT"

It was a dark and stormy night and I was looking forward to relaxing on my sofa and reading an exciting and frightening novel.

I had just made myself comfortable and selected "The Werewolf of Notre Dame" when the telephone rang.

'Sarah?"

"Alice?"

"I've seen him!"

"Seen who?"

"Tom, my husband!"

"That's impossible Alice; Tom's been dead for three months."

"It's him though; I know it is, he was looking in the window."

"Alice, you're hallucinating. It's just your nerves."

"Sarah, could you come over? I'm really scared."

"OK Alice, just hang in there. I'm on my way.

I didn't tell her I had already dressed for bed and that I really was not looking forward to getting out in the driving rain but Alice had always been there for me. She was a godsend when Ben, my husband died and I couldn't let her down now.

The short five mile drive seemed to take forever. The rain peppered against the windshield and even though I had the wipers at their maximum speed, I had difficulty seeing the road.

Finally, I pulled into the long driveway. The old farmhouse had been well kept and when her parents died she had inherited it. Being the only child she sold off all the land with the exception of several acres on which the house set.

I ran to the porch as fast as I could and called out Alice's name as I knocked on the door.

She opened the door and fell into my arms.

"Alice, calm down. You know it can't be him and you know he can't hurt you anymore."

"But I think the police are suspicious because his brake line was cut. Sarah, I do well to fill up the tank with gas. I wouldn't know where the brake line is."

"I know and I think they know that too"

"But they know what a bad marriage we had and that he was always beating me."

"Do you want me to stay with you tonight?"

"Please, if you don't mind."

That night Alice told me stories about the five years of her marriage with Tom that even I didn't know. The late night parties he would have with his drinking buddies, the women they would pick up, the drugs they used. When Tom came home he would take it out on Alice.

As I stood up to get a drink of water, I glanced out the window. The rain was still coming down. I let out a scream and dropped the glass. There staring in the window through the rain was Tom. I looked at Alice who had turned pale. Quickly we turned out the lights. I looked again but the figure had disappeared into the night.

That night neither of us got any sleep.

You know it can't be him. Tom was cremated. His ashes are in the mausoleum.

"But it is somebody," Alice said. "You saw him too."

"Yes, I did but there has to be an explanation."

"Sarah, what am I going to do? If I call the police and tell them I saw my husband who's been dead for three months, they're going to send the paddy wagon to pick me up."

"Well, why don't you just tell them there's a peeping tom [oh, sorry about that], I mean someone who has been looking in your window and that you live alone and could they swing by every once in a while and check on the neighborhood?"

Alice decided that was a good idea and after giving them a general description of the man she and I sat down to talk.

I asked Alice how much she knew about his family. Did she ever meet any of them?

She said he was born in Quinton, a town about fifty miles away and that his mom and dad had both died when he was young. He was raised by a friend since his parents had no close relatives but she never met her.

"Do you remember her name?"

"He just called her Flossie. Never told me her last name. I know, you must think I had to be naïve to not ask more questions about his past but I never once thought he was anything but what he said he was. In the six months we dated he was so thoughtful and kind. It was only after we were married that he became abusive."

"Sarah, I hate to ask you, but could you stay with me for a while, at least until we find out what's going on?"

"On one condition, that we go to Quinton tomorrow and try to find this Flossie that raised Tom. Maybe she can clear up some things."

Alice agreed and the next morning we headed for Quinton.

Quinton was a small town of about 400 people. It was off the main highway and had one main street that sported a grocery store with a small pharmacy. Next door was a hardware store and across the street was an older building that advertised antiques and junque spelled with a q.u.e. at the end. Next to the antique store was the gas station with an attached maintenance garage.

Good place to start our quest for Flossie if she actually still lived there I thought. I pulled in to the drive and we both got out of the car. In the garage was a sixtyish, gray haired man who looked like he hadn't missed any meals. He greeted both of us with, "Well, what are you two stylish ladies doing in a place like this?"

"We're looking for a lady named Flossie. We don't know her last name but she took a boy by the name of Tom Malkim to raise when his parents died."

"Flossie, Flossie." The man rolled the name around in his mouth. "About how old would she be?"

I looked at Alice.

"Maybe close to 70?" Alice nodded in agreement.

"I've been away for a long time but there's a lady who used to be a nurse whose name is Florence and they sometimes call her Flossie who lives over on the hill." He pointed to a house in the distance. "Her last name is Fletcher. She lives by herself and uses a walker. She's always home but give her some time to get to the door because she moves real slow."

We thanked him and drove to the house to which he had indicated.

The house was Victorian style in bad need of paint. A wrought iron fence enclosed the house. We opened the gate which squeaked as we pushed it aside. The porch was a wrap-around with a ramp built over the three steps that led to the porch and the front door.

I rang the doorbell and we waited.

Finally the door opened and before us stood a petite, white-haired lady. The lines in her face seemed to match her age I thought. It was a kindly face and one I would associate with a person who took care of people. She was dressed in a pale pink housecoat.

She greeted us with a friendly smile and ushered us to the couch. We introduced ourselves and when we told her the reason for our visit, her countenance darkened.

"I tried so hard to get through to Tom," she started, "but I failed him. Oh, he was good, good at manipulating people, good at making them believe he was this most wonderful caring individual but when he got what he wanted he was ruthless. I'm glad they separated the boys. I wouldn't have been able to handle them both."

"He had a brother?"

"Yes, actually he was a twin."

Alice and I looked at each other in shock

"Do you know where his brother lives?"

"No, I don't know who adopted him and I never heard from him. If he's like his brother, I'm sure he's up to no good."

We told her what had happened the past week and while it still frightened us, at least we were pretty sure Tom had not risen from the ashes. But why would his brother try to frighten Alice?

We thanked Flossie and drove back to town

Alice was still worried about staying by herself so I said I would be glad to stay as long as she needed me.

It had been misting all the way home but when we pulled into Alice's driveway the skies opened up and the rain came down in torrents along with the thunder and lightning. The wind was swirling the rain everywhere and by the time we reached the door our clothes were soaked even though I had used my umbrella.

We took off our wet clothes and Alice handed me one of her housecoats.

"I'm going to make us some hot tea," she said as she headed over to the stove.

As Alice went to the sink to fill the tea kettle she let out a scream. "It's him, its Tom's brother. He's right outside the house."

Just then a flash of lightening filled the sky and the house went dark.

"Oh no the electricity is off. What are we going to do?"

"Quick, call the police." I said

"I don't know the number," she said panicking.

"Just dial 911," I said, "This is an emergency."

Alice dialed the number and a lady answered. She gave the address and then the phone went dead.

"He's cut the line," she screamed. "We have to hide."

Just then we heard a loud banging on the door. Alice and I were both hiding behind the couch. Alice had grabbed one of her heavy vases and I grabbed the wet umbrella.

The pounding on the door got louder and louder.

"I don't think he can break down the door, do you?" Alice whispered.

All I could say was, "I hope not."

The thunder and lightning continued unabated and so did the pounding on the door. Suddenly we heard a loud crash against the door and listened as it gave way to the impact of the huge wrought iron statue that was standing on the front porch.

We could make out the outline of the figure as he came through the splintered door. Dripping wet he made his way inside his flashlight in hand. He waved it around the room and moved closer to the couch. Just then he shined the flashlight behind it where we were huddled together shivering from fright.

As he stood over us I aimed my umbrella and stabbed at him as hard as I could. It knocked him down but he quickly got up. I kept poking and Alice hit him as hard as she could with her vase smashing it over his head. It stunned him for a second but he grabbed Alice and knocked her down. I kept poking at him with my umbrella. I was not about to let go. Just then I heard the sirens of the police. He heard them too and ran out the door.

They caught him in the front yard, placed the handcuffs on him and came to see if we were OK.

Several days later we were notified by the police that Leo was looking for the drug money that Tom owed him. He confessed that he had cut the brake lines to cause the accident that killed Tom. Once again Tom had fooled Alice into thinking that he was anything but what she had married.

The police came to question Alice about the drug money but she convinced them she knew nothing about it.

However, I must confess that didn't keep us from doing some really deep house cleaning, from top to bottom and if we ever find it you might just see us somewhere on a tropical beach, enjoying a Pina colata and looking for romance.

IT WAS ORANGE

"It was red."

"It was not, it was orange. I know it was orange. I saw her run out from behind the house right after I heard the shot and the dress was orange."

"Well, I was watching through the binoculars and I could see her really well and I know it was red."

Emma was incredulous. "What were you doing spying on the neighbors through the binoculars?"

"I wasn't spying, I was watching the birds. Did you know we have a Yellow-bellied Sapsucker in our yard?" Hattie asked defending herself.

"Well I was in the front yard and I saw her real clear and it was orange," Emma continued, "I saw her get in that orange car."

"It looked red to me." Hattie said.

"Well, it was orange. You know you've always been colorblind," Emma said emphatically.

Hattie chose to ignore Emma's last remark. She knew who was colorblind and it wasn't her.

"We need to call the police because there might be a body around the back of the house." Emma continued. "You call them and I'll go over and see what's going on."

This time Hattie decided to flex her verbal muscle and tell her sister she did not think it a good idea because it might be dangerous and, too, she shouldn't disturb the crime scene if there was one.

Emma agreed with Hattie that she was probably right even though she liked to think of herself as an amateur detective.

So while they waited for the police to arrive Emma told Hattie that she would tell the police what they saw because if Hattie contradicted her statements about the colors it would just confuse them and she reminded Hattie again that she was the one that was color blind.

The two sisters had lived together in the same house all their lives. They had never married. They took care of their parents until they passed away. Their father made sure none of their suitors ever made it to first base with his girls. Now they were both in their seventies and if there were any men available they would be so frail they would probably have to be carried or rolled down the aisle in a wheelchair. So the two sisters found themselves alone with each other. Emma was younger by two years but was definitely the stronger personality. Hattie let her lead although her feelings were sometimes hurt.

When the police arrived Emma took full charge. She gave them all the information she had and insisted on following them over.

They found the body of what appeared to be a middle aged man in the back yard. He had fallen on his back. He was dressed in a brown tweed suit and his face sported a graying neatly coiffed beard and mustache. It appeared he had been shot once in the head. A pool of blood had spread out from behind the victim's head.

The policeman turned to Emma. "Do you know the man?"

"No, he just moved in a couple of weeks ago. I took some cookies over to welcome him to the neighborhood but he didn't seem too friendly. He said 'Thank you' and closed the door, never even gave me his name."

"Ok," the policeman continued, "tell me again. What kind of a car was it?"

"I don't know the kind of car it was except it was small and it was orange. I know it was orange because her dress was orange and it matched the color of her dress." Emma said emphatically.

"Well, thank you very much." he said. "If we need anything else we will be in touch."

Emma felt very smug and satisfied with herself. She was glad that Hattie hadn't tried to interject her ideas into the conversation. It would only have confused the policeman needlessly.

Several days later Emma noticed the police car in front of the victim's house.

Emma didn't hesitate to go over to find out what progress had been made. She gingerly opened the front door and called out a "Hello."

The policeman came to the door. Emma asked what progress they had made and whether they had found the car and the woman.

He stated that she had been found and the murder involved a child custody case but couldn't say any more about it because it had not yet gone to court.

"Oh by the way, you told me the car was orange. It was really red. Just thought you'd like to know." he stated as he walked back into the house.

Emma stared at the retreating figure and then said to herself, "I can't believe how many people are colorblind."

"KATE"

Not a day goes by that I don't think of her. Not a day goes by that she isn't on my mind, that beautiful young lass with the flowing red hair. She was a lovely moment caught in time and God allowed me to share a few of them with her.

I first saw Kate one balmy spring morning as I was driving to the village. The windows of my car were down to catch the refreshing breezes. In the meadow to my right I noticed a flock of sheep following the bellwether. Walking beside the bellwether was this lovely petite red-haired beauty.

I stopped but she paid no attention to me. I wanted to call out but decided against it.

The next morning I drove by and stopped again just for a while. I repeated the same scenario a number of times and each morning she and the bellwether led the sheep to the pasture. She could not help but see me but still chose to ignore me. Finally, one day she looked my way. I waved a big wave and smiled a broad smile. She came over to the fence where I stood and smiled a shy smile. She seemed even smaller and more frail than she had from a distance. She said very little when I tried to engage her in conversation. I had the feeling that her young life had not been all that happy.

I learned very little about her except that she lived with her mother. She pointed to a house barely visible from the road.

I knew I had to go slow. I suggested some morning that I bring a basket of food and that we enjoy a picnic in the meadow while watching the sheep. She agreed.

The day was perfect, a few fleecy clouds in an azure sky. We sat under the tree enjoying the sandwiches I had made while listening to the birds and watching the butterflies flit from flower to flower.

Why did I have this longing to be with her always? Why was I falling head over heels for a fragile child I hardly knew? I called her a child because she told me she was twenty and here I was turning thirty. But she held me in her grip, and I couldn't let go.

I asked if I might meet her mother. At first Kate seemed reluctant but I was persistent and finally she gave in.

When I drove up to the cottage, Kate came out to meet me. The cottage was small and quaint. The furniture was sparse but adequate. Kate introduced me to her mother, Angelica. I could see where Kate came by her red hair. But her mother was a large woman with weathered features. She bore none of Kate's fragile looks. I wanted to make a good impression so I enthusiastically extended my hand. She hesitated but finally offered a limp hand. I chose to ignore the cool reception. I was not going to let it get me down

It was an awkward situation because Angelica said less than Kate did. I think Kate noticed how uncomfortable I was and suggested we go out into the garden. She looked at her mother for acceptance and her mother nodded that it would be all right. Why this twenty-year-old woman would have to get her mother's approval to go out into the garden was another of the mysteries I encountered with this family.

Kate led me out to the garden. There before me was a profusion of herbs. I recognized some of the more ordinary ones, such as, peppermint, spearmint and chocolate mint just by rubbing their leaves in between my hands. I also recognized the lemon balm, oregano and thyme.

"My mother grows all kinds of herbs," Kate offered.

"What does she use so many herbs for?" I asked.

She chose to ignore the question.

I wanted to get to know as much about her as possible. I wanted to become her confidant. I wanted her to trust me, but she was not letting me share her life-at least not yet.

In the ensuing weeks we did grow closer, and I sensed she was not well. I felt Kate was afraid of her mother because when the three of us were together there was a certain pall that hung over the entire scene. Angelica seemed to have some strange hold over her. It was like Kate was a victim of some strange form of malaise.

I thought the best thing for Kate was to get out from under the influence of her mother.

"Will you marry me?" I asked Kate.

"I need to ask my mother." she replied.

"Kate, you're a grown woman old enough to make up your mind. Why can't you just say yes? Does she have some hold over you? Look, we'll go ask her together, ok?"

Much to my surprise Angelica thought it would be a good idea. I was relieved because there was definitely something creepy about this place.

On the day of the wedding clouds were threatening rain. I can remember my mother saying if it rained on your wedding day your marriage would be stormy and troubled, but I was too excited to let it bother me. At last she would be my wife, and we could spend the rest of our lives together.

The guests arrived and each moment I waited for her to come seemed like an eternity. We waited but Kate never came.

"What have you done with her?" I demanded of Angelica. She ignored my question.

She told the minister to dismiss the people and motioned for me to follow her in my car.

We drove back to the house. After getting out of our cars she led me back of the house, past the herb garden and down a path that led into the woods.

There we found Kate, her body hugging a small stone. I ran up to her. Her body was still warm, but her pulse was weak. I lifted her frail body off the stone and as I did, I noticed the name "Patrick" which had been roughly etched into it.

"Who's Patrick?' I demanded of her mother as I carried Kate to the car.

Angelica suddenly seemed contrite.

"It's all my fault." she confessed. "I forced her to abort her baby. She never got over it. She felt she was a murderer and didn't deserve any happiness. But I couldn't let her carry the child. It was her father's. He raped her but she still wanted to keep it. I forced her to take the herbs. She insisted on burying the baby, even though he was not fully developed. So we put it in a little box and dug a grave in the woods. We said a prayer over him but she just couldn't let go."

"Where's her father?" I asked.

"He committed suicide. His grave is farther back in the woods. She never got over the two deaths. I'm so sorry it came to this."

Angelica held her daughter all the way to the hospital. I took Kate from her arms and rushed her into the emergency room. They worked with her for several hours, but it was too late. The doctors did not have to do an autopsy because Angelica knew Kate had taken an overdose of the same herb she had forced her to take to abort her baby. How ironic it is that the herb that killed both Kate and her baby is the same name as her mother, Angelica.

Not a day goes by that I don't think of her. Not a day goes by that she isn't on my mind.

MOTHER WOULD BE PROUD OF ME

My name is Sarah Lee and before you ask the obvious question, no I am named after my aunts not the gal who bakes the pies and cakes and my name has an h on the end of it. I live in a comfortable neighborhood, two-storied house and the good-looking kid down the street mows our yard. I live with my mom and dad; a dog named Homer, who hates the mailman and a cat, Chester, who snores.

It was a good life until my parents decided to get together and add to the family. Now at the age of thirteen I am stuck with a brat of a brother who I get to baby-sit while mom goes to her never-ending meetings and dad goes who knows where. They named him Harry Cain. My friend has a gerbil named Harry and I don't know what they were thinking of when they came up with Cain, you know the guy in the Bible who killed his brother. I call him Hurricane like a big windstorm that's always wrecking things. That's pretty much what he's done to my life. At first I didn't mind sharing the limelight with Hurricane but after a while I realized I had become a second class citizen in my own house. I decided I had to do something about it.

One day I got a brilliant idea. Hurricane, who's now 11 months, is always into everything and I always have to clean up his mess. This time I decided to take him out of his cage, I mean playpen and let him loose. Hurricane was just starting to walk and mom had a pretty candy dish on the coffee table.

"Look, Hurricane, a pretty dish," I said pointing to the intended sacrifice. "Wouldn't you like to hold it?"

He hurried over to the coffee table half-crawling, half-tottering and grabbed the dish. Crash! On to the floor. Good job Hurricane, I thought as I checked to see if he had cut himself. No cut, but I could still put a big Band-Aid on him and tell mom how I kept my baby brother from bleeding to death. Then I put him back in his cage and cleaned up the glass. I would make sure I told mom how I tried to stop Hurricane but that he was just too fast for me. Mother would be proud of me. And she was.

The other night mom and dad came home late in a lovey-dovey mood after dining out and went upstairs to their bedroom and closed the door. Oh how I hope this doesn't mean I'm getting another brother in nine months. Anyway the next morning after they had both gone and left my brother and me at home I went into the bedroom. Sure enough, mom had left her shoes and stockings on the floor. Seeing another golden opportunity I called to Homer who came bounding up the stairs. I tossed the stockings at his feet and he did what all good dogs do, proceeded to shred them. I thought better of having him trash her shoes so I put them away. When she came home I would meet mom at the door and tell her how Homer had nosed his way into their bedroom and shredded her stockings before I could stop him but that I saved her shoes. Mother would be proud of me. And she was.

Another one of my duties was to feed Chester and make sure he had water. No problem, he slept most of the day. Well, you know how cats love yarn and Chester was no exception, when he was awake. One day mom left her yarn halfway exposed in the bag. Times were getting tough again and I was being ignored. I needed to take action. With cat in hand I guided Chester to the yarn and stuck it out a little farther. He came to life. Grabbing the yarn with his claws Chester went twisting and turning the yarn in his paws, running through the house and thoroughly enjoying the romp. I had to literally put him outside to get it away from him so I could try to roll it up in a ball. When mom came home I would tell her that Chester found the skein of yarn she had left out enough for him to grab and that I had to take out all the knots and roll it up in a ball. Mother would be proud of me. And she was.

I realize eventually my brother will be able to talk and I will have to change my strategy. The dog will one day go to dog heaven and have all the stockings and shoes to chew on that his teeth can handle. The cat will either run away or go to cat heaven where he can bury himself in balls of yarn. Hopefully in nine months we will still be a family of four. Until then I will keep trying to remind them how important I am to this family and that they can't get along without me.

MY CHANCE MEETING

I caught sight of him in the distance-at least I thought it was him. How long had it been since we last saw each other? It must have been five, six or maybe even seven years. I was hesitant to go closer. I tried not to appear too excited but I edged ever closer until I could get a better look. He seemed to be distracted and didn't notice me. "I'm positive that's him," I said to myself.

My mind drifted back to the wonderful times we had spent together. I remembered the dark summer nights when I would spread a blanket down for us on the soft grass and we would drink in the celestial beauty of the stars. I would point out the Milky Way and inform him that noted astronomers were sure there was a black hole in the center but not to worry because we were situated in one of the spiral arms of our galaxy and would never be sucked in. Then I would point out the Northern Cross or Cygnus, the Swan as it was sometimes called. I would further bore him by pointing out some of the other constellations. On nights, when Mars, Jupiter and Saturn were in the sky, I would explain to him that you could tell the difference between a star and a planet because a star would twinkle. This was because of the tremendous distance from the earth but planets did not because they were so close to the earth. He would just look at me and never say a word.

In the cool of the morning we would go for a walk in the meadow where the daisies were blooming. I couldn't resist picking and plucking the petals-he loves me, he loves me not.

If it came out he loves me not, I would pluck until it came out right.

We never went to movies or concerts but we enjoyed many evenings, just the two of us, watching TV. I would pop popcorn and we would snuggle on the couch. Sometimes he would fall asleep, especially if it was a boring movie.

All these memories were precious to me and I really missed him. When he left I asked after him but no one had seen him. It was as though he had vacated my entire life. I mourned for a time and friends tried to comfort me. He's probably found someone else. You can always find another. I thought, that's easy for you to say. You didn't know him like I did. How can you find a replacement for a dear friend? I remained alone all these long years and now he was back

I edged closer. Should I call out his name? Would he remember me? Would he want to come back to me? Could it be the way it was before? Had he changed in the years we had been apart? All these questions raced through my mind while I stood there watching him. Finally I decided it was now or never. I had everything to gain and nothing to lose.

"Orville," I called. He turned toward my voice. Then he sat down. I walked slowly over to him. "Orville, where have you been all these years? I've missed you so much." But he just sat there and didn't say word. Isn't that just like a cat.

MY ROOMMATE

We were asked to write a story using the following words: tennis shoe, M & M's, dust bunny, backscratcher and period. This is the result.

Now don't get me wrong, I like my roommate, Theresa. To say she's a bit strange does not do justice to the word. I mean anyone who mixes rhubarb with sauerkraut and eats it too is in a category all by herself.

Anyway, I was lying down on the couch having fallen asleep dreaming of basking on one of the exotic South Sea islands in a bright red bikini {OK, so I didn't always have this figure, and besides, it was a dream} and watching the most gorgeous sunset ever, when I felt a sharp pain in my shoulder.

"Wake up!" a voice screamed. When I finally got my eyes open, I saw my roommate standing over me looking as though she had just killed a man.

"I think I've just killed a man," she screamed jumping up and down and pointing to the door.

I looked down at her feet. She was only wearing one tennis shoe.

"Where's your other tennis shoe?" I asked ignoring her last remark which had still not registered with me.

"Didn't you hear me?" she screamed again. "I said I think I've just killed a man."

"Oh come on, Tess, {that was what we all called her}, what are you talking about?"

"Well, just as I got out of my car, this guy across the street started running toward me. I got scared and threw the flowerpot at him. I hit him right in the head."

"You hit him with my aloe-vera plant?"

"Well, I couldn't just let him attack me, could I?"

I felt kind of bad, putting my aloe-vera plant before my roommate. "Of course not," I said, "I'm sorry."

"Let me get the flashlight and put on my shoes and we'll see if he's out there." I felt under the couch for my shoes and drew out one huge dust bunny.

Ok, now is not the time to remind her it's her turn to run the dust mop.

After I found my shoes, I picked up the flashlight and a baseball bat we had just for such emergencies and told Tess to wait by the door with the cell phone ready to call 911 if I should find him out there.

I turned on the porch light, gingerly opened the door and walked across the porch out to the yard. I saw the broken pot and the aloe-vera plant on the ground.

"Did you say he came almost up to the front porch?"

"Yeh, right up to the front steps."

"Well there's nobody here now." I shined the light to the ground where the broken pot and plant lay. I found her other tennis shoe in the grass close by and saw what could have been a few drops of blood. However, I didn't feel safe spending any more time outside. I grabbed the tennis shoe and hurried back indoors.

"I think we should make a report to the police." I said

"But what should I tell them?"

"Tell them you thought he was coming to attack you and you hit him in self defense."

So Tess called the police who came out to take her statement. While they were questioning her I decided to fix some dinner for us since we were both hungry. This time I would fix the mashed potatoes myself and take out my portion before she added the M&M's to them. I told you she was odd.

Later that evening, I sensed she was still uptight so I drew a tub full of warm water for her and poured in some of her favorite bubble bath.

"Just sit in the bubbles as long as you like, it will do you a world of good just to relax." I thought to myself, that's really what she needs.

After a while I heard her call. "Fran, would you bring me my back scratcher, please?"

I thought that's good, she's feeling better.

I took the back scratcher to her and started to gently scratch her back.

"Fran," she started again, "you know, it was really kind of odd."

"What was odd?" I asked.

"Well, one of those policemen they sent over."

"Yeh, what about him?"

"He had his head bandaged up."

Period. End of story.

MY SCARECROW

I had always wanted to live in a Victorian house with a wraparound porch and now was the time to take advantage of that situation. When I received a promotion in my job it required me to move to Vermont. I decided on a sleepy little town of 5000 inhabitants and that included the cats and dogs. It would only be a twenty-minute drive to work and away from the hubbub of the bigger city. The realtor was very helpful and had just the house I wanted. It was on the corner with a vacant lot on the south and only one neighbor next to me. It seemed to be a quiet street with very little traffic and down the street on either side were rows of brilliant red maples shining in the morning sun. What an inspiring sight! The only down side was a detached garage but that would still keep my car out of the snow and cold winter.

The month of October in Vermont was everything I had heard it was. The red of the maples, against the contrast of the evergreens was breathtaking. As I drove around the little town, it was amazing how extravagant their decorations for Halloween were. Though I was busy moving in my new house I felt compelled to at least put up a scarecrow. On the side of the house, facing my neighbor's lot was a flower garden filled with mums of every color. It was a perfect spot to put the scarecrow

At the local nursery I bought a bale of straw and stuffed some of it in the sheet that I had sewn together. In the back yard I found several tree limbs and tied straw around them for arms and legs. A pillowcase stuffed with straw would serve as the

59

head and I decided he should have a scowl on his face to make him look fierce. Now my scarecrow needed some clothes. I didn't really want to use my clothes on the scarecrow because I had only brought good clothes with me, but luck was on my side. While taking some boxes up to the attic I had spied some clothes over in the corner. There was a pair of pants, large, dirty and stained, also a plaid shirt in the same condition. I handled them gingerly. I probably should have used gloves but my hands were already dirty. They were perfect for a scarecrow. I looked up in the rafters and hanging from a nail was the perfect straw hat-it already had holes in it. After assembling and dressing the scarecrow I placed it in the flower garden and stepped back to admire it. Not bad I thought-not bad at all.

I had not yet met my neighbor but one morning while out in the yard, I saw him leaning over to pick up his newspaper. I called a cheery, "Good morning, How are you?" but he didn't acknowledge my greeting. Instead, he seemed to stop, glared at my scarecrow, turned without answering, headed toward the door and slammed it behind him. OK, so it wasn't a work of art. It was the best I could do with what I had and I didn't make it for him anyway. That kind of bothered me, but I thought, well, maybe he just isn't a morning person.

Well, as all you women know, and some men too, we eventually need to find a hairdresser. I was determined to find one in the neighborhood who could tell me all the gossip because, let's face it, this is the number two reason we go to the beauty shop. I found one. Her name was Sophie and she was a talker. She was also a native of the town and knew everything about everybody. Talk about hitting pay dirt.
Actually, she told me more than I really wanted to know. I knew the previous owner was Carl Wilson and that he had died. What I didn't know, that she told me, was they found him hanging from the rafters in the garage.

"They said it was a suicide. But frankly, I got my doubts," she added.

By now, I was thinking about hanging my real estate agent for keeping that little tidbit of information from me but I ask Sophie, "What makes you think it was murder?"

"Well," she continued in her own particular style of English, "they didn't find no chair close to Carl's body when they found him. Now how did he hoist hisself up into that noose?"

"Didn't the police investigate?" I asked.

"No, he didn't have no family and nobody cared, 'cause him and Harry was at each others throats all the time." At that point she let out a big belly laugh. "Get it, throats, rope, hanging?" I smiled; I didn't want to encourage her.

"Who's Harry?" I asked.

"Why he's your next door neighbor, Harry Jenkins." She replied, surprised that I didn't know.

My thoughts went back to my real estate agent and what I would like to do to her. "Tell me about Harry."

"Well," she started enthusiastically, "they was both widowers. While their wives was alive, they was civil to each other, but after they both died they argued about everything. Harry didn't even come to Carl's funeral."

 "So, is he harmless?" I asked, wondering seriously if I should start looking for another place.

"Oh, I think so; at least we ain't had no more hangings in town." She let out another belly laugh and I made a mental note to look for another hairdresser. "He's just not friendly and don't have no friends." she added.

I made it home with a fairly decent perm and decided I would give Harry all the room he wanted. I looked over at my neighbor's house just in time to see an older lady come out. Should I wave at her and risk being snubbed? I decided that she looked pretty friendly so I waved and called "Hello." To my pleasant surprise she waved back. I introduced myself and she told me she came in each week to clean the house for Mr. Jenkins. We engaged in trivialities and finally I got up enough nerve to ask her about Mr. Jenkins. She agreed he wasn't the easiest man to get along with but he did pay well and she needed the money. I can't tell you why that made me feel better but it did.

One morning I looked and saw the right arm of my scarecrow had been torn off and was lying on the ground. How could that have happened? I picked up the arm and stuffed it back in the sleeve. I didn't put too much importance in the incident but the next morning both arms had been pulled off and were lying on the ground. I attributed it to pranksters and figured it was something I would have to put up with, especially around Halloween. One night, the head was knocked off and its legs were broken. This was too much. I decided I would stay up and find out, once and for all, who the tricksters were. It was difficult to stay awake but about midnight I saw someone come out of my neighbor's house. As the figure came closer, to my great surprise, I could see it was Harry Jenkins. "What is he doing here?" I whispered to myself. Then I saw him go over to my scarecrow, tear off the arms and legs and completely dismantle it. He seemed like a wild man, it really frightened me. Oh fine, I thought, now I live next door to somebody whose elevator doesn't go to the top floor. I couldn't get much sleep that night but I made up my mind that the next morning I would talk to the police.

The next morning I looked over at my scarecrow expecting it to still be dismantled but to my surprise it was standing up good as new. How strange I thought. Maybe he felt bad about it and decided to put it back together. Then I noticed something even stranger-the police were next door at Harry Jenkins house. One of the officers was standing outside. "What happened?" I asked.

"A lady that does housework for this guy found his body this morning. Looks like somebody strangled him. Did you know him?"

"No, I just moved in. He didn't seem very friendly." I responded.

"Yeh, I heard nobody liked him."

"Do they suspect anybody?" I asked.

"No, but it's the darndest thing-they found straw on the floor by his body."

At that statement, cold chills went up and down my spine. I excused myself and went over to get a better look at my scarecrow. On its face where I had painted a scowl there was now a faint smile.

MY UNBELIEVABLE ORDEAL by Claude Pigeon

I will never again look into the heavens without fear in my heart. Fear in my heart for not only me, but for the friends I have left. I will always think of those who disappeared into this huge abyss never to be seen again. I will always wonder about their fate.

They call me Claude and what I'm about to tell you will make your hair stand on end. It certainly made my feathers poof out.

First of all, I need to tell you I'm a homing pigeon. A good one too. I've never been lost or even confused.

The day we set out on our 93-mile flight was as clear a day as you could imagine. The trip normally took about two hours. It was a race that we routinely made, really a piece of cake. As we flew into the heavens, we filled the sky like 2000 tiny white clouds. I'm sure it was a very impressive sight for those below.

Homer and Horace were in the lead. They always were. I flew close to Claudette. She and I were planning a family soon.

We were flying along, not wasting time, but still not flying so fast that we were not able to enjoy the checkerboard pattern of the landscape below and the houses with trees protecting them from the harsh winters.

Suddenly, the sun, which had been shining brightly, grew dim, like a big cloud had covered it. I looked up. All I could see was something huge hovering over us. It was not a cloud and it was closing in on us. I could see that the group was panicking. I still did not recognize what it was until the belly of the beast started to open. Then I knew that we had encountered a UFO, an Unbelievable Feathered Ornithogiganticthropedus. There were stories about these flying monsters but nobody had ever seen one. My Aunt Gertrude had warned us about them. She insisted they were from another planet. All the pigeons thought she was nuts, a bit cuckoo, if you'll pardon the pun. Nobody paid any attention to her. Now I realized she knew what she was talking about. But this one was not real; it had been designed, possibly by pigeons from outer space.
I watched as Homer and Horace were the first to be sucked into the monster. The other pigeons that were flying close to them were literally swooped up in a mass.

I looked at Claudette and motioned with my wing to change direction, but she couldn't keep up, and I watched helplessly as she disappeared into the UFO. As I started to fly after her, the belly closed and the monster sped off with unbelievable speed.

More than half of our group was gone. How were we going to explain this to the pigeons back home? The flight home was long and sad. There was a crowd waiting for us when we arrived. But as soon as they saw us and that many of the group was not with us, they began to bombard us with questions.

"Where's Homer? Where's Horace? I don't see Claudette." All of them were chirping their questions at the same time.

I motioned for us all to go to the Pigeon House. When we were all gathered and settled I looked around. I saw Penelope who was sitting on her nest. Perry was beside her. He was one of the lucky ones who had not made the flight. I also noticed Henrietta, Horace's mate. Now her little ones that were just born would never have a father. A tear came to my eye.

"Fellow pigeons," I began when they had all settled down, "I don't know where to start. The story I have to tell you will seem so incredible that you may not believe me, but trust me it is true and the pigeons that returned with me will back me up." They all nodded their heads in assent.

I told them how our flight started routinely, that the day was beautiful but suddenly the sky was darkened with this monstrous flying beast.
One of the young pigeons interrupted me.

"Oh! Oh! D-d-do, do you mean an Unbelievable Feathered Ornithogiganicthropedus?"

I looked at little Sylvester. I couldn't believe he had heard of this monster that most of us thought was just a myth. I could only suppose that he had heard it from his mother, who had heard it from my aunt. Well at least we wouldn't call my Aunt Gertrude cuckoo anymore.

"You're quite right, Sylvester." I responded and patted him on his head.

His eyes opened wide. "Can we go see one?" he asked excitedly.

"Son," I started, "you don't want to come close to one. They open their belly and suck you inside. I don't know what happened to our friends."

At that statement, little Sylvester grew quiet and moved close to his mother.

"I don't want to frighten you, but now that we know this monster actually exits, we must always be vigilant."

I don't know what lies in store for us. We will certainly have to be more watchful. Some of us may go on strike or demand hazardous pay. We will definitely demand more feed and better living quarters.

Then I remembered a science fiction movie I saw when I was young. It was called "The Thing from Another World." A UFO had crashed in the arctic. A reporter and a small group of scientists were sent to investigate. The Thing came to life and terrorized them until they finally destroyed it. In the end the reporter said the most dramatic words, which I repeated to my fellow pigeons. I raised one wing toward the sky and with a dramatic tone in my voice, I chirped loudly, "Watch the skies, keep looking, keep watching the skies."

MY VERY UNUSUAL VACATION

I could hardly contain my excitement. I was on my way to my first vacation in five years and it wasn't going to cost me a thing.

You see, I had entered this contest, not ever thinking I would win. However I thought, if I don't enter, it's a sure bet I won't win.

A month later I received a notice in the mail to call this 1-800 number. I had just won an all expenses paid trip to the Bahamas for four days and three nights. I could hardly believe my luck. These things just don't happen to me. I hastily dialed the number. The lady on the other end gave me options. I could either take the trip or the money. Now I know, a lot of people would say, "Take the money," but I really felt adventurous, so I said I would take the trip. Not only would they fly me there in their private plane but they would pick me up at my door and take me to the airport.

Of course, I had to go shopping and buy some beautiful clothes for the trip. After all, you never know whom you might meet and you certainly want to look your very best. I came away with three pairs of Liz Claiborne shorts and matching tops and an evening skirt slit up to the thighs. Then I saw a pair of sandals by Liz that practically ran over to me and said, "Buy me," which I did.

Well, the big day finally arrived and this stretch limousine pulled up in front of my house. I thought, "Neighbors, eat your heart out."

The driver rang the doorbell. I let him in and he grabbed my bags and carried them out to the limo. I looked to see if any of my neighbors were watching. My next door neighbor, Carol, was out in the yard with her dog. I yelled to her, "See you when I get back from the Bahamas." She waved back but didn't seem too excited. She's probably green with envy I thought.

My luggage was loaded on the plane and we took off. On the way down, I was served a fantastic meal and watched a movie giving info on the Bahamas. There are seven hundred islands that make up the Bahamas. Forty of them are inhabited. I briefly entertained the thought that maybe I could find a contest that would offer an island as a prize. I was really feeling lucky and thoroughly rested when we set down at the airport.

We drove to the hotel, and I was checked into a spacious suite. I unpacked, relaxed and later that evening was treated to another fabulous meal. I was thinking I probably should have bought clothes that were a size larger.

The next day they drove me down to the dock. "We have a very special treat for you today," I was told. "Today you are going to cruise the beautiful Caribbean. We have provided you with this elegant yacht and your very own expert navigator. All you have to do is just enjoy the day. We've stocked the boat with enough food for a picnic on one of the many islands you will see while you are on your cruise."

Just then my navigator stepped off the yacht. My mouth flew open. I mean, he was built like a god. He was an Adonis. He was dressed in shorts, no shirt and was rubbing suntan lotion on his heavily muscled arms that glistened in the bright sun. He looked like Mr. Universe, I kid you not. His thick blonde hair was short and wavy, streaked by the sun. He reminded me of a blonde Rock Hudson.

"This is Jeffrey," I was told. I'm sure my mouth was still wide open but I did manage a weak "Hi."

Jeffrey smiled and waved at me. "Jeffrey will be your navigator. He hasn't been with us very long but he says he knows these waters like the back of his hand."

We pushed out of the port and headed for open sea. I sat watching him guide the yacht.

Later, I got up the nerve to ask him, "Do you think I could steer sometime?"

"Maybe," he said, casting a quick glance in my direction.

So he's the strong silent type, I thought. I'll just sit back and relax.

As the day grew on, I noticed some clouds starting to gather. In fact, I could see a huge dark cloud looming just above the horizon.

I wondered if I should say something to Jeffrey but they did say he knew this area like the back of his hand. I decided not to worry about it.

However, my concern grew because we seemed to be heading straight into the ominous looking cloud. The wind began picking up and the waves were dashing against the yacht with growing ferocity. Jeffrey was having trouble steering the craft.

It's silly the things you think about at a time like that. I was remembering the song from Gilligan's Island. "The weather started getting rough. The tiny ship was tossed. If not for the courage of the fearless crew, the Minnow would be lost."

Well, I couldn't speak for Jeffrey, but I wasn't feeling brave, in fact, I was downright scared.

It seemed like an eternity that we were being tossed aimlessly in the open sea. Then suddenly, there appeared an island up ahead.

Jeffrey tried his best to steer for the land, and we were fortunate that the wind was blowing us in that direction. I prayed we would get there before the boat fell apart.

Finally, we were tossed on to the rocky beach. The force with which we landed though tore a gash in the side of our yacht.

The impact caused me to hit my head on the seat. I put my hand up to my head to see if there was any blood. I was relieved to find none. Jeffrey was still at the wheel.

Well, at least we were safe, but Jeffrey who "knew this area like the back of his hand," had no clue where we were.

So we stayed on the yacht until the storm abated. The sun was shining low on the horizon. I looked at my watch, 7:00pm. I checked to see if the second hand was still moving. It was.

I turned to Jeffrey. "What should we do? Can the boat be fixed?"

"I don't know." That was not what I wanted to hear.

"Well, don't you have a radio? Can't you call the coast guard, or the shore or somebody for help?" I asked, getting a bit irritated and also a bit concerned for my safety. After all, he was a stranger to me and they said he had not been working there very long.

Jeffrey fiddled with the radio and tried to call out but there was no reply- only static.

"Surely they'll come looking for us. We were supposed to be back by now," I reasoned.

"Yeh, they'll find us." He seemed completely unconcerned about our plight.

At this point I was getting more frustrated than scared and I probably asked a question I shouldn't have asked. "How often do you get lost in these waters that you know like the back of your hand?"

He just glared at me.

We decided we should disembark and walk out on the rocky shore. The island didn't look inhabited but there was a dense forest of trees and underbrush beyond the shore.

The sun was setting and I really didn't think it was a good idea to be out of the boat long because there could be wild animals roaming around just looking for supper.

Then Jeffrey came up with what he thought was a brilliant idea. "Let's build a fire. Then when it's dark they'll be able to spot it." I say brilliant because we had just come through a near hurricane, everything was wet, and we're supposed to build a fire.

"We can pour gasoline on it. There's bound to be driftwood on this beach somewhere. Why don't you go and look for some?"

"Why should I go? Why don't you go?"

He started limping toward me. "I sprained my ankle. I don't think I could walk on this rocky ground."

I looked at him. Why did I ever think he looked like an Adonis? Right now he looked more like a Don Knotts.

I stumbled over the rocks mumbling under my breath when suddenly I heard the roar of a plane. I looked up. They had sent a seaplane to search for us and had spotted our yacht on the shore. They landed as close as possible and helped us into the plane. Jeffrey said he needed help because of his sprained ankle. I was still suspicious.

I spent the rest of my vacation on the island. They were very apologetic about the unfortunate situation that had befallen me, through no fault of my own, and gave me an extra sizable sum to spend. I think they were afraid I might sue them, but I'm really not the suing type. However, they didn't know that and I didn't bother to tell them. I accepted everything they offered. I bought lots and lots of mementos, and I dined at some of the finest restaurants until I almost felt like I was taking advantage of them.

And what about Jeffrey? I guess I was really lucky. When we reached the port the authorities were waiting for him. It seems he was wanted for embezzling money from an older widow woman who had befriended him.

Oh yes, I noticed when they led him away, he didn't limp a bit.

Next time I win a contest for a trip or money, I am definitely going to take the money. I'll just redo my whole house. It will be more fun.

REST IN PEACE, AUNT LIL

I stared down into the coffin. She looked so peaceful. They did a good job on her head, I thought.

"I'm so sorry." Her friends came up one at a time to console me. "Such a tragic accident."

Mary, her good friend, said, "I told her she should have put a light in the basement, but she wouldn't listen. I told her she was going to trip and fall sometime and break her neck."

I nodded in agreement.

"But I don't think you should have buried her in that bright red dress. The Lord may not recognize her."

"She wanted it that way," I replied. "She always told me red was her favorite color."

My parents died in a skiing accident and left me an orphan at the age of five. Aunt Lil, my mom's sister, took me in and now at the age of sixteen I found myself alone again.

Aunt Lil tried to give the appearance of being quite prim and proper. We went to Church and Sunday school every week. In fact, Aunt Lil taught a Sunday School Class for young married couples, even though she had never married. Nobody seemed to mind this incongruity.

Aunt Lil was very strict. She insisted I let her know what I was doing all the time. I felt stifled. She seemed to watch my every movement. I tried to bring my girlfriends to meet her but she was very abusive to them. There was one girl I really liked. No, I was in love with her. Allison was her name. I called her Allie. Aunt Lil seemed to hate her more than most. I had a feeling she was jealous.

I saw Allie as much as I could. We decided we had to get away as soon as possible. Her parents didn't care where she went. They would probably be glad to see her leave and I needed to get out from under Aunt Lil's thumb.

We set the date. She was supposed to meet me at the station but she didn't show. Her parents seemed indifferent to her disappearance. I did not mention it to Aunt Lil but I watched her to see if there was any change in her attitude. There was nothing I could detect, except she seemed to be drinking a little more. Drinking was one of her secret vices she guarded carefully.

"Go down and get me another bottle, Alex," she would say. I grabbed the flashlight and carefully descended the damp concrete steps. While down there, I shined the light onto the massive metal door on the far wall. When I had asked Aunt Lil what was behind that door she became angry and screamed. "It's none of your business and don't ever ask me again."

She would really have been upset if she knew I had seen her sneak downstairs with her male friends.

One night I hid in the basement and watched her open the door. I saw where she hid the key. The next day, while she was away, I took the key and unlocked the massive door and pushed it open. A foul smell invaded my nostrils. I trained the flashlight along the wall but the batteries were weak. I couldn't see very well but I spotted a table and carefully made my way over. On the table, I could barely make out candles and a knife. Beside them was an open book. I felt some matches and lit the candle just as something brushed against my leg. I dropped the candle and screamed as the cat jumped up and dug its claws deep into my arm. I felt the blood run down. I hit the cat as hard as I could. It let out a loud hiss and ran away.

I groped for the candle, which had gone out when it hit the floor. The batteries in my flashlight were completely dead. I felt around on the floor and finally found the candle. As I rose up, I bumped my head on the table. Fumbling for the matches, I relit the candle. The smell was getting stronger. I held the candle high. My hands were shaking almost uncontrollably. On a larger table I could make out the naked body of a young girl. Now I knew where the stench had come from. I drew closer. Her chest was covered with blood, now dark and clotted. Her face was swollen, but I still recognized her. It was my Allie!

Hatred swelled up within me like never before. When Aunt Lil came home that afternoon, I called to her from the basement.

"Come here," I said, "I have something to show you."

She grabbed a flashlight and started down the steps.

"What are you doing down there?" she demanded.

She didn't wait for an answer. As she reached the bottom of the steps I hit her with a board. It caught her off guard. She tried to defend herself but I was stronger. I dragged her body back up the stairs and then threw her back down.

I told the police she had lost her balance on the slippery steps. They didn't seem to question my story. I never told them about the secret room. It didn't seem necessary. I finally feel free, and I know Aunt Lil will never rest in peace. You see, she hated the color red.

THE CARNIVAL CAME TO TOWN

The kids in town were all excited-the carnival was coming to town. Billy, next door and his friend Alex had strung a rope on the highest limb of the old oak tree in the yard for a trapeze. At least the highest limb that mom would let them climb. Alex pretended that his dog Harvey, a Cocker Spaniel, was a lion and kept trying to get him to set up on the retaining wall so he could show his expertise in taming the savage beast. Unfortunately, Harvey would have none of it and ran for cover.

As I watched, I remembered with sadness the last time the carnival had come to our town. It was almost five years ago to the day when my brother disappeared.

Sam was twelve at the time, five years younger than me and I have missed him so much. Not knowing what happened to him hurts more than seeing him dead and knowing that at least he is free from pain. My brother was a free spirit from the time he was born. He and I were great buddies and we did many things together but for some reason mom and I could never understand, dad was never happy with anything Sam did. Dad would beat Sam for no reason at all. Regardless of how hard Sam tried to please him, dad could always find some reason to use his belt on him. Mom and I tried to do what we could to make up for the abuse and anytime I could take Sam somewhere away from dad I took the chance. So when the carnival came to town I thought this would be perfect. Sam would love seeing the wild animals, the sideshows and everything else that went with the event.

When we arrived at the fairgrounds all the tents and makeshift buildings were set up. It was as if Sam was in a different world. He was off and running.

"Meet me back at the entrance in four hours." I yelled and pointed to my watch as he sprinted off to high adventure. That was the last I ever saw of Sam. I waited at the entrance for hours and searched all the tents and asked the people at every sideshow but no one had seen a twelve year old boy that fit Sam's description.

Mom blamed me at first but realized that Sam probably took this opportunity to run away from what must have seemed to him like an impossible situation. He did not realize the impact it would have on my mother and me. We tried to find him but I think in our hearts we realized that we would not find him and we hoped that wherever he was his life was more pleasant than it had been at home. Dad took to drinking and one day he too just walked out of our lives. Mom decided not to bother looking for him.

I really wasn't excited about going to the carnival but decided that it was not the fault of the carnival that my brother disappeared. I tried to get mom to go but she would have none of it-she did blame the carnival.

It was crowded and I did find myself getting caught up in all the hype and attractions of the day. I caught sight of Billy and Alex trying to pop balloons for a prize. I thought to myself, "The tips on those darts are probably blunt-they'll never win." But as I watched, Billy popped each balloon he aimed for and won a huge water cannon. I walked over to congratulate him. "I guess I had better be on my guard from now on-right?" I joked.

"O Mary, you know I'd never use it on you." he insisted. Billy was a good kid and I knew he was serious.

I walked down to the less congested area just to get a look at some of the people behind the scenes who make up the circus. A clown was looking in the mirror while he was putting on his makeup. Suddenly he turned around, "Mary?" I looked at him. "It's Sam! He exclaimed. "I'm Sam your brother!"

I stared unable to speak. Five years had added a lot of growth to his frame. He was now taller than me. "Sam! I can't believe it's you. Have you been with the circus all these years?"

"Yes." Sam replied, "And I love it. This life is so exciting. It's everything I've ever wanted."

We stood there hugging and kissing for a long time.

"You have to see mom. She has been so worried about you but she knows why you left."

Sam hesitated and I quickly informed him that dad had left us several years ago.

"Then I will come home with you as soon as I finish with my performance."

After Sam had made the kids laugh with his antics Sam took off his makeup and we headed home.

"Better let me prepare mom for the surprise." I said. "I don't want her to have a heart attack."

As I walked in the door I told mom, "I have a surprise for you. It's someone you haven't seen for five years."

Mom's eyes became as big as saucers and she almost ran over me to get to the door. She knew who I meant. They kissed and embraced each other for a long time then stood back and sized each other up to see how the lost years had treated them.

It was the most wonderful thing that could have come out of the carnival. First it seemed to take my brother away and now it brought him back.

Neither mom nor I tried to get Sam to leave his life with the carnival. We knew that Sam had found exactly what he was looking for and that made everybody happy.

THE MARRIAGE OF BUGSY AND FLORA

"Over my dead body!" yelled Felix Flealeone.

"Then that's what it'll be!" yelled back Bugsy Buglieri.

Felix was the head of the Flealioso Family in the prestigious suburb of Flatsville.

Bugsy Buglieri, on the other hand, lived on the other side of the tracks and was, as Felix said, a pain in the-you-know-what.

But now their two babies, as they both referred to them, were grown and wanted to get married.

First of all, who ever heard of fleas and bedbugs marrying? That in itself was ridiculous.

Felix was outraged. After all, his Flora had studied to become an interior decorator. Her floral arrangements were something to behold. Everyone lovingly referred to her as Flora, the Flower Flea.

But Flora was also wayward and strong willed. One day she had spied Bugsy, Jr. lifting matchsticks he found along the railroad tracks. She had never seen anything like him before. Strong and handsome, that's what he was, not like those wimpy fleas her parents always wanted her to date. She was smitten with the, pardon the pun, bug.

Busgy, Jr. also spied Flora out of the corner of his eye. He too fell head over heels for her. He piled more matchsticks on his back than he ever had, to impress Flora. Their eyes finally met. They didn't say a word but she smiled a big smile. Bugsy smiled too even though his back was killing him.

That afternoon, Flora went home with stars in her eyes and Bugsy went home with a backache. But he, too, had stars in his eyes.

The next week Flora's mother, Fiona, noticed a big change in her daughter. She was bouncing off the dogs like crazy and singing, "That bug of mine."

Fiona felt Flora surely meant to say flea instead of bug so she didn't give it another thought.

Meanwhile, Bugsy's mother, Beulah, also noticed a change in Bugsy. He was helping her without even being asked. She knew he must be in love. When she asked who the lucky bug was, he would only say, "You'd be surprised."

Each night Flora and Bugsy, Jr. would meet down by the railroad tracks. Bugsy would lift more and more matchsticks until Flora could hardly see him. Afterwards he would throw them up in the air to the delight of Flora. He would then flex his muscles and she would run over to ooh and ah over his fabulous display of strength. She would tell him he reminded her of Arnold Schwarzenegger. Bugsy would throw out his chest with pride. Well, fleas and bedbugs DO watch TV too, you know.

When they would meet down by the railroad tracks, Bugsy, Jr. would pull up a pebble for Flora to sit on. She always marveled at his strength. Then he would pluck a blade of grass and lift it over his head and cover the pebble for a cushion.

One night Bugsy, Jr. surprised Flora. He had worked all day at fashioning a piccolo by drilling holes in a matchstick with a pin he had found on the ground. Bugsy, Jr. loved the classics. After practicing all day, he thrilled Flora by playing "The Flight of the Bumblebee," flawlessly. After this Flora could not contain herself. She gave Bugsy, Jr. a big hug. Unfortunately, the barbs in their arms and legs got locked together. For a while it looked as though they would be there until someone came to rescue them, but Bugsy, Jr., having a scientific mind, lifted his legs and arms as Flora lowered hers and they were able to disengage. However, being young, adventurous and full of fun, they made a game of it. As they unlocked, they would say he/she loves me, he/she loves me not. Of course, they made sure they ended with he/she loves me. Later, they decided it would be better to throw each other a kiss.

Well, as we stated earlier, Felix was not too happy about Flora and Bugsy, Jr.'s relationship. As head of the prestigious Flealioso Family, Felix felt that Flora could do better. However, Bugsy, Sr. had no problem with his son marrying up in the world, which he felt was what he would do if he married Flora. Bugsy, Sr. really liked Flora.

Flora did what most females do. She went to her mom. If she could persuade Fiona, she knew her mom would be able to talk Felix into letting her marry Bugsy, Jr. At first, Fiona was against the marriage but when Flora told her how much fun she would have being a grandmother, Fiona made Felix his very favorite dinner plus his very favorite dessert of chocolate cream pie. He finally gave in.

So Flora and Bugsy, Jr. were married down by the railroad tracks. Felix even gave them a lavish honeymoon at an extravagant hotel on the right side of town. As luck would have it, Bugsy, Jr. found the matchbox that had housed all those matches that had meant so much to him and Flora. With his mighty muscles, he moved it to a place Flora had always dreamed of living.

A little while later Flora gave birth. She named the girls Flora 2, Flora 3, Flora 4, Flora 5, Flora 6, Flora 7, Flora 8, Flora 9, and Flora 10. The boys, Bugsy, Jr. named Jr. 2, Jr. 3, Jr. 4, Jr. 5, Jr. 6, Jr. 7, Jr. 8, Jr. 9 and Jr. 10.

We're not quite sure what you would call the kids of a flea and a bedbug but we thought fleable was kind of cute.

Well, Flora and Bugsy, Jr. don't have too much time to themselves now but when they do, they still go down to the railroad tracks. Bugsy Jr. still plays the piccolo he made out of the matchstick but he is more mellow now. He plays the slower tunes like "Down By the Old Railroad Tracks" and "When You and I were Young, Flora." Just for kicks Bugsy will play "The Old Gray Bug, She Ain't What She Used to Be," and Flora will sing it in her soft sweet voice.

Well, this is the story of the courtship and marriage of Flora and Bugsy, Jr., and we're happy to report that they lived happily ever after.

THE BEAR AND THE RACCOON
An Aesop's style fable

The bear was walking through the woods when he heard a voice behind him.

"Mister Bear, where are you going?"

He turned around to see a fat raccoon following him.

"I'm going to my secret place," the bear replied.

"And where would that be?" the raccoon asked moving up beside him.

"Can't tell you it's a secret."

"Oh, I love secrets and your secret would be safe with me."

"But if I told you it wouldn't be a secret."

"I promise I would never ever tell anyone about your secret place, honest. People have told me lots of secrets and I have never told anyone any of them."

After much pleading and assuring the bear he would never breathe a word the bear finally relented and said, "Ok, but you really can't tell a soul."

The raccoon nodded. "I promise."

They went deeper into the woods and finally came to a huge oak tree. The bear started climbing with the raccoon close behind him.

The bear came to a hole in the trunk of the tree. He stuck his hand in the hole and pulled out a huge clump of honeycomb dripping with honey. The bear moved aside to allow his friend to share in the bounty. All afternoon they ate until they were stuffed. The raccoon left again and assured the bear that his secret was safe with him.

The next day the bear went to his tree to enjoy a meal of honey only to find the raccoon and his friends up in the tree taking turns pulling the honey out of the hole.

Furious, the bear yelled up at the raccoon. "You promised me you wouldn't tell anyone where my secret place was."

"I know," the raccoon said licking the honey off his hands, "but you should realize that the only way a secret will remain a secret is to keep it to yourself."

THE CROW AND THE DUCK-BILLED PLATYPUS
An Aesop's style fable

"Hot stuff, hot stuff wow I IS hot stuff!" the crow crooned to himself. Turning himself in as many positions as possible he admired the beautiful creature in front of the mirror someone had left propped up against the trunk of the tree. As he hummed to himself and drank in his perfect form, his eyes narrowed in to something else he saw in the mirror. The crow turned around and out of the pond crawled one of the weirdest looking creatures he had ever laid eyes on.

He approached the animal, "Yo dude, what did yo' mama sleep with? You is one ugly puppy"

Unperturbed the platypus looked up at the crow. "I'm a duck-billed platypus and yes I get that comment a lot but let's face it you're not exactly Hollywood material."

"Whoa, wait a minute. You see my beautiful black shiny feathers?"

"So what," the platypus shot back. "I have beautiful soft fur that graces my entire body."

Well the crow was not to be out done. "Look at my graceful legs," he said as he strutted back and forth.

"Graceful?" the platypus laughed. "They're so skinny; I'm surprised you can stand up on them. My legs are short and I have fingers and toes to grab my food with."

"Well," replied the crow getting a bit defensive, "whatever is growing out of the end of your face is just about the ugliest thing I have ever seen."

"Yeh, but I can put a lot more in my bill than you can with that skinny one that's coming out of your face."

By this time the crow was getting so upset if his feathers had not been black they would have been turning red with anger.

"Look," the platypus finally said, "let's face it, you were made to do the things you do and I was made for the things I do so let's call it a draw and part friends."

The crow thought for a moment. "You're right and I have to admit you're so ugly that you're really kinda cute."

The platypus also admitted that even though the crow was full of himself, he did command an air of dignity.

THE SHOES

I did it; I can't believe it's mine! The old homestead is finally mine. I had waited so long to buy the farm where I was born and spent 18 years of my life. It had been sold and rented several times. The last renters were two months behind in their rent. The owner lived in another state and when he sent the sheriff to collect he found the renters in the barn making methamphetamine. They were arrested and taken to jail. The sheriff confiscated all the material and at this point the owner decided it was the time to sell. The time was right for me too.

It may be hard to explain how someone could become so attached to a piece of the earth but I had so many fond memories of the woods on our 104-acre farm. The woods where I sat at the edge of the creek to paint and compose my silly poetry-I wanted to recapture them again.

When I moved in I knew some things would be changed. The front porch where I used to sit in the swing and try to catch the sunbeams, which I later realized was dust waiting to land on the furniture, had been closed in but I would address that later. Now I wanted to take a look at the farm that was so dear to me.

As I walked through the gate and started down the hill things didn't look too different. The milk barn, the milk shed, chicken house, and corncrib-they all looked the same.   The barn where the sheriff discovered them making meth looked the same but as I edged farther down the hill my heart sank. The upper pond where we seined fish was a dry depression covered with weeds. Farther down, the lower pond was in the same condition. Dad had dammed it up to hold in the water. I made my way through the brambles that stuck to my clothes and the tall dried weeds that snapped as I tried making it to the natural spring below the pond. The spring fed a creek and there were three massive stone steps that led down into the spring. I continued down to see if the giant stone steps were still there. To my delight, they were. Oh, how I wished the farm could be like it was when I was young.

I made my way back up to the barn where the renters had made their illegal drugs. This was the barn where the farm machinery had been housed. The massive doors were ajar and as I peered in I could see all the machinery had been removed. I stepped in and looked around. I climbed the ladder up to the loft. Straw had been put down on the floor. I wondered if they had slept here when they were stoned out from inhaling the meth. As I scanned the loft, my eyes saw something over in the corner. I crawled over to the object. It was a pair of shoes like a court jester would wear. They were multi-colored; the front curved up to a point with a tiny bell on the end. I thought how weird but I picked them up and took them with me. I wondered if they would fit me. They seemed almost new. Should I try them on? Why not, what have I got to lose?

The material they were made of was soft and leather-like. I laughed as I put them on-they looked so funny but they were a perfect fit. As I put on the last shoe, my head started spinning and the scene around me grew blurry and I slumped to the ground. I felt weak but soon the feeling passed. Something felt different. I pulled myself up and looked around. Down the hill the upper pond was filled with water, the grass was green and mowed short. The lower pond was also filled with water and I was able to walk down in the new-mown grass. The water in the creek below the pond was flowing over the stone steps just as I remembered it when I was a child. How can this be? It had to be the shoes but what magic did they possess? The trail down into the woods was cleared and I easily walked down the path. How many times I had longed to return to my youth and now I had the means to do so. I wondered how the shoes knew where I wanted to be. It must have been when I wished the farm to be as I remembered it when I was young. Could I wear these shoes forever and would the farm always stay the way it was now? I headed back to the house. Would the front porch be open as I remembered? There were cattle in the field and chickens roaming the farm just as I remembered. It was so surreal. I looked out over the hills. I was sure I saw dad plowing the field in the distance. I ran home as fast as I could. I was sure I would find mom cooking in the kitchen. But as I ran the shoes started to come apart and disintegrate. At the same time my fairy tale world started fading. I found myself looking at the same farm that I had seen when I first arrived.

The shoes are gone and I have no idea what they were or where they came from but for a wonderful brief moment in time I was able to recapture the past I had cherished so much.

THE STRANGER

This was the only picture I was able to take of Michael. I grabbed my camera just as he was climbing the steps to his cottage. As I did, I tripped on a big rock. I held tight to the camera but was only able to catch the bottom of his legs.

I had moved out to the country, away from the hustle and bustle of the big metropolis because I feared for the safety of my two children, Jamie, 8 and Regan, 10. The city had become place of violent crime, and I felt the country would offer a safer environment.

The world was in a state of turmoil and had been for a long time, fighting on so many fronts and with very little hope of it ending soon. My husband had been one of the first casualties, leaving me with children to raise. Jamie and Regan were good kids, and I wanted them to stay that way.

Through a friend, I found this small house which would do for our family. A small room that had been built on the back would be perfect for my art projects.

It sat at the bottom of the hill. The front of the yard was planted in a profusion of shasta daisies, lupine, dianthus and various kinds of primroses. The back yard was level for about 100 ft. before it ascended the hill. The hill was forested with evergreens and maples that reached into the sky, blotting out the sun. The environment was just perfect for tall healthy ferns, and I guessed that the previous owner had planted the hosta that grew huge along the hillside.

At the top of the hill sat a little log cabin. I asked my real estate agent if anyone lived there-I thought the kids might be able to use it as a playhouse. She informed me my property only went to the edge of the bank. It was actually rental property, and an older gentleman had moved in several weeks ago.

The next few days we were busy moving our meager belongings into our new home. I looked up occasionally to see if there was any activity at the cabin on the hill. Jamie and Regan were curious too. They wanted to go up by themselves, but I convinced them it would not be a good idea. After all, we didn't know anything about him. For all we knew, he might not like people, he might have guns, and he might be a criminal, a pedophile, who knows. By now, I was beginning to scare myself so I didn't say any more.

One day, though, I looked up and saw our neighbor. He waved at me. That gave me the sense of confidence I needed, so I gathered my young troops and set up the hill. There were only about a dozen steps dug out in the rock. The rest of the way was a long narrow path leading up to the cabin.

As I huffed and puffed my way closer to our destination, he stood outside waiting for us. He had a thick shock of white hair and a ruddy complexion leaving me to assume he probably spent a great deal of time outside. He had a kindly face, something like the grandfather I wish my kids had known. I judged him to be about 5 ft. 9 inches. He removed his sunglasses and reached his hand out to me. As he did, I noticed his eyes. I have never seen anything like them. They were absolutely magnetic. They were so intense. They were every color bursting as if in a cosmic explosion. I felt like I was witnessing the birth of the universe. I looked at the children but they didn't seem to notice anything out of the ordinary. Is it me I wondered, am I hallucinating? Am I the only one that sees this? He noticed my startled expression and quickly put the glasses back on his eyes.

"Welcome" he said as he laughed, "it's quite a climb. My name is Michael. Come in and rest awhile. It won't be so hard going down."

I introduced myself and Jamie and Regan as he ushered us into his cabin.

It consisted of one large room. Next to the sink was a table and chairs. A bunk bed was over in the far corner. A pot-bellied stove in the center of the room heated the cabin. I surmised he used the stove for cooking too. On the floor were books and magazines. I tried to read the titles but couldn't make them out.

I saw no food, which compelled me to inquire if he needed anything. He smiled and shook his head. "All my needs are taken care of and you are very kind for asking. I live a very simple life as you see, but it is all I need."

Jamie and Regan took an instant liking to Michael, and for some reason, I felt they were completely safe with him. Before we left he invited us to come visit him some evening. "You can't imagine how close to the stars you feel up here," he said smiling. "The Andromeda Galaxy seems so close you feel you can almost touch it."

After that, Jamie and Regan went up often. "What do you do up there?" I asked. "I don't want you wearing out your welcome."

"Michael says we can come up any time we want to. He helps us with our homework. He's a genius. He knows everything about everything." Regan took the initiative to tell me.

Not to be outdone, Jamie told me that he had some awesome pictures of galaxies, and he had this telescope that could show you right where they were.

I was glad he was such a wonderful influence on them. I was really getting concerned that their grades were suffering because I was not able to spend as much time with them as I would like.

One afternoon, while the children were still at school, I became tired of staring at my canvas. I decided to bake some cookies and take them to Michael to show my appreciation for all he had done for my boys.

I knocked on the door and called to him. When Michael came to the door he was not wearing the sunglasses. I saw the same violent explosion in his eyes I had witnessed the first time. It startled me. "Your eyes," I started, but he put his finger up to his mouth as if to stop me from asking. "You will understand soon. Please don't worry. Everything will be fine."

Meanwhile, the war was not going well. Many of our soldiers were dying and people were becoming discouraged.

I kept busy with my art, and the boys continued to go up and visit Michael. One day they came down and told me Michael said he would be gone by the next morning.

"Where is he going, how is he going?" I asked. "Is he going by plane? Does he need a ride to the airport?" I had never seen a car or any kind of transportation anywhere close to the cabin.

"He says he has everything taken care of." Regan offered. He said we will have a pleasant surprise in the morning.

Both boys held up a small, beautiful marble box. "Look what he gave us," they said proudly. "He told us we couldn't open it until morning or it would spoil everything."

That night, after the boys were in bed, I couldn't sleep. I went outside to get a look at the stars that Jamie and Regan had become so fascinated with since their association with Michael. Michael was right. They did seem so close away from the glare of the city lights.

I was half-asleep in my lounge chair when I noticed a light in the northern sky. As I stared, it grew larger. It looked exactly like the explosion I had witnessed in Michael's eyes but a thousand times more powerful. The light came down and seemed to land behind the cabin. I couldn't make out any activity, and I wasn't about to go up to the cabin to investigate. I felt I had just seen a UFO. I watched for a few minutes and soon the light lifted up and disappeared into the night. I had difficulty going to sleep that night, but I knew if I didn't, I would get nothing done the next day.

The next morning I awoke bleary eyed and turned on the TV to find out a truce had been negotiated between the warring parties. Our soldiers would be coming home soon. It was the day for which many of us had prayed.

Jamie and Regan were up early - after all it was Saturday and they didn't have to go to school.

The boys were excited and came running with the little boxes Michael had given them. When they opened them they exclaimed. "He left it! He told us he would give us both one!"

"Well, what is it? Let me see." Inside each box was small, perfectly round sphere that was exactly like what I had seen in Michael's eyes. It was pulsating, exploding into all different colors.

"But what is it?" I asked. "Did Michael tell you?"

"Yes Mother," he said, "this is how the universe was created. This is the eye of God."

THE TIN CUP

Sam was the fifth child born to Pete and Clara Foster. They were looking forward to an empty nest but one night of revelry was all it took and viola, Sam. To make matters worse he was what the politically correct might call slightly mentally challenged. In a family of bright siblings that had accomplished outstanding grades, Sam really threw a monkey wrench in their plans which were to do some traveling when the last of their four children planned go to college next year. Sam at ten years of age would be dependent on them for another eight years. To make things worse Sam craved attention and when it was not forthcoming might get in all kinds of trouble. It's not that he was mean or bad, it's just, along with being a slow thinker, he didn't have much common sense either.

Enter Uncle John, Clara's brother, who really took a liking to the lad. They seemed to share a common bond of friendship and understanding. Uncle John had given Sam the only real present he had ever received. When Sam was five Uncle John had presented him with a tin cup and on the bottom was engraved "With Love to Sam, Uncle John." Sam carried it with him constantly and finally Uncle John gave him a leather cord so he could tie it around his neck. John told him he would have to take it off at night because he might choke. Sam refused to take it off the first night but after almost choking to death Sam put it on the night table so he could put it on the first thing in the morning.

John had recently retired from work and was spending more time with Sam and before he realized it Sam was practically living with him. This didn't bother John because he had never married and had no children. He enjoyed the company. John lived on the farm alone and was really glad to have Sam as company.

Sam had always wanted a puppy. His parents said no because they knew with Sam's limited ability he would never accept the responsibility of its care. John knew of a farmer who's Golden Retriever had given birth to a litter several months ago and so Rufus became a part of the family.

Sam and Rufus played together constantly but Sam always made sure that the tin cup stayed around his neck. Rufus was good company for Sam and John also knew he would protect Sam. They shared many things together and John would wince when he saw Sam letting Rufus drink water from his tin cup. Oh well, he told himself, if I hadn't seen it I wouldn't know about it and who knows what else they do when I'm not there.

John home schooled Sam but Sam was more interested in running with Rufus. Some days he and Rufus would hunt for rabbits while John tended the garden. John tried to keep track of them as much as possible though.

Clara and Pete never came over to see how Sam was doing but it didn't bother Sam-he had Uncle John and Rufus and his tin cup-the first present he could ever call his own.

Finally Uncle John decided that Sam should be capable of menial work and inquired of his friend Tom at the feed store.
"Tom, would you have anything that Sam could do down at the feed store? You know his limitations but I think it would make him feel good if he could work and save up a little money."

Tom thought for a minute, "You know," he started, "I could use someone to stock and load sacks of feed. I think he would be good at it."

"He's a good worker," John stated positively. "He'll do anything he can for you."

So Sam reported for work the next day with Rufus by his side. "Now go back boy," Sam ordered Rufus. "I'll see you when I get home."

Everyday Rufus walked Sam to work and later as Rufus learned Sam's hours Rufus would be waiting to walk Sam home.

One day as Rufus came to meet Sam there was a crowd gathered around the store. Rufus waited for Sam but he did not show up. Finally, Uncle John went over to Rufus. "Come on home boy we won't find Sam here."

A burglar had held up the feed store demanding money from the cash register. Sam had tried to fight the burglar off but had been shot in the chest. Sam was taken to the hospital where he died the next day. Rufus could not understand where his friend had gone until Uncle John brought Sam's body to the farm and buried him where he and Rufus loved to play. Uncle John made sure that the tin cup was buried with him-after all he should never be without it.

Every day, Rufus goes to Sam's grave and lies there to mourn the boy who let him drink from his tin cup.

WHEN YOU COME TO A FORK IN THE ROAD, TAKE IT

I once had a friend who was wise tell me, "When you come to a fork in the road, take it." Well, that opportunity came to me one day as I was out walking. I came to a fork in the road and I took it. It had four tines and a porcelain handle. I picked it up and to my sheer horror and amazement it started squirming.

"Let me down" it shrieked. I dropped it like a hot potato.

"What do you want from me? I was just resting and now you've disturbed me."

I was still in shock and couldn't answer.

"I know, I know what you want. You want me to take you to all the finest restaurants and treat you to all the most scrumptious food in the world. Right?"

I managed to shake my head in the affirmative.

"OK, just follow me."

As we trudged down the road his tines making small clouds of dust as they touched the dry ground, he continued,

"Now I only do desserts. The dish ran away with the spoon and the knife just couldn't cut it but I promise you, you won't be disappointed."

Me, disappointed? I felt this either had to be a dream or I had died and gone to heaven.

In no time at all we were in a French restaurant luxuriously decorated with cute little fat cherubs and, for all practical purposes, naked ladies.

The waiter came over to the fork, "Ah Monsieur Fourchette, it is so good to see you again. It has been a long time."

"Yes," the fork sighed. "You'd be surprised how many people don't take the fork in the road."

"My friend," continued the fork, "will have the Profiterole au Choclat."

When the waiter brought the dessert it was a huge cream puff filled with vanilla ice cream and topped with a rich chocolate sauce.

I felt like a queen and to think I was eating with a magic fork.

After thanking the waiter the fork transported me to a German restaurant where I enjoyed a large slice of Black Forest cake layered with butter cream and sweet cherries. And of course no visit to a German restaurant would have been complete without homemade apple strudel topped with whipped cream and a side of ice cream.

By this time I was starting to feel a bit full but I was so amazed at what was happening that I didn't want it to stop.

An Italian restaurant was our next stop. As we entered, our eyes beheld a huge mural of Pompeii with Vesuvius looming large in the background. My fork seemed to know every waiter in each restaurant we visited and they greeted it with a hardy hello.

The fork ordered me a Tiramisu-Mascarpone custard layered with whipped cream and rum and coffee soaked lady fingers. And of course I had to have Spumoni-an Italian ice cream with chocolate, cherries and pistachios.

I was glad I had elastic in my slacks because I could feel the band getting tighter. Next stop, Spain. The fork ordered me a flan, a vanilla egg custard topped with caramel sauce.

At this point I decided to address the fork and let it know unless it wanted me to be sick that we should not order any more desserts.

"Our next stop is the beautiful island of Hawaii," the fork stated totally ignoring my plea. There it ordered me a Hawaiian cake topped with vanilla pudding and whipped cream. It was practically being forced in to my mouth.

"You will love our next…." At that point I grabbed the fork. It squirmed to get away but I held tight. With my free hand I grabbed a stick and started digging a hole. I dropped the fork in the hole and covered it with as much dirt as I could find. The fork tried to get out of the hole but I piled on more dirt and held it down until it remained quiet and I was sure it would not get back up.

Was it a dream? I found myself in bed. It was light outside. I glanced at the clock -8:00 o'clock. I crawled out of bed, made my way to the bathroom and stepped on the scale. I had gained seven pounds. It wasn't a dream after all.

Right then and there I decided I had a new mission. I had to find and bury all those forks in the road so no one else would be tempted to pick them up ever again.

JESUS
an Acrostic

Just as Jesus battled Satan
Even as God saved the Israelites
Should we not battle that Dragon too?
Until Christ comes again
So we can spend Eternity with God

A CAT CAN BE A THING OF JOY AND COMFORT
An Acrostic

And to all who love animals
Could there be anything sweeter
At which our hearts melt in us
Than a kitten soft and cuddly?
Could we give our love to something cuter?
And make the days go by faster?
No, I could not live without a cat
Because the days would be so dreary
Even the sun would not shine as bright
And the stars would seem to fade
The flowers would not be as beautiful
How could life mean as much?
It would be a dull existence
Nothing would give us such joy
Going though life would be no fun
Oh, who would share our joy and sorrow?
Fill our life with endless pleasure?
Just as I know God created us to love
Our lives were meant to share
Yes, our love with all God's creatures
As we continue down life's road
Noting as we go
Doing the best we can
Caring for the earth and all that's in it
On our way to the final goal
May we freely express our love and blessing.
For the four-legged companions we have known
Of that need we all must give
Reach out to them whenever we can
To return that love they so willingly share

A DAY IN MY LIFE

When I awake in the morning and the world is fresh and new
I first consult my calendar to see what I must do
Bake cookies I have written, but who do I bake them for?
I don't bake cookies for myself, at least not anymore
Could it be for a picnic, or maybe a bazaar?
I need to call a friend of mine, my memory needs a jar
Now where are my glasses, I had them last night?
I put them on the desk but they're nowhere in sight
I'll go downstairs and see what I find
I know I've left them somewhere behind
Oh, there's the telephone, "hello," I say.
"No, I don't want a time share, thank you, good day."
Now I've lost my train of thought
Did I come down the stairs for naught?
But what it was I can't remember
I'll go upstairs to spark an ember
Oh, I remember now, my glasses are gone
I'll check to see if I have them on
I feel my forehead, that's a relief
'Cause my kids are always giving me grief
About being forgetful and losing things too
So I don't tell them half the things that I do
I'll bake the cookies and get them done
And surely later I'll find someone
Who can tell me where they're suppose to go
So the number of cookies won't be too low

I hear the repairman at the door
He's been here four times before
My dehumidifier is on the fritz
That's what he's been trying to fix
The first time he tightened the screw on the fan
But it still sounded like a rusty old van
The next time he had to order a switch
It was cracked when it came, now isn't that rich?
So he ordered another, I opened the box
The box was so big and the part was so small
I looked at the paper and found nothing at all
I shook the paper-the part fell to the floor
Oh, if I break this they'll really be sore
Well here's my repairman again, my weekly friend
We're on a first name basis now but I wish this would end
I'm sorry he says after making the repair
You need a new motor, the noise is still there
I'll see you next Friday, have a good week
I smile a weak smile, what should I think?
This could go on forever, it makes my heart sink
Well. On with the day, there's plenty to do
It's not even lunchtime and I'm not nearly through
I call my neighbor, "How about a walk?"
"Sounds like a winner," she says, "let's walk and talk."
We walk down the street and soak up the sun
Taking it slow 'cause she's 91
There's a persimmon tree up on the hill
Every year the neighbors get their fill
We pick the persimmons that fall to the ground
Each year the fruits just seem to abound
We're fortunate the owner doesn't mind
Otherwise we would find ourselves in a bind
We thank the lord for the bounty given
By this majestic tree that stretches toward heaven
That afternoon I check my fridge
To find what leftovers I can see
A grilled cheese sandwich I settle on

That sounds good enough for me
When evening comes, I watch TV
The history channel makes my day
Egypt, ancient mysteries and UFO's
As I sit down to crochet
So that is the extent of one of my days.
They are never all quite the same
But if each day were like the other
I would only have myself to blame

AN AUTUMN WALK

As I walked along a pathway on a sunny autumn day
A host of fiery colors met my gaze along the way
The leaves of red and gold and brown
Did a sky dance 'round my head
I smiled while watching their descent
To a leafy winter bed
I wondered at the beauty of the brilliant autumn hues
It almost took my breath away, so many lovely views
How did God plan such beauty for this body to behold?
How could he be so gracious to share a gift worth more than
gold?
And as I walked I pondered the many blessings of my life
About how God had cared for me through happiness and strife
So I must make good use of autumn so when winter comes to
call
I won't regret that I didn't take more inspiring walks this fall

A TRIBUTE TO MOTHERS

This is to mothers everywhere,
Those who are dark and those who are fair
And even to the mothers who opted
And allowed their little one to be adopted
And given the home they could not provide
This is love seen from another side
For giving up what they love is brave
So their child will have the family they crave
And to those who stayed up when their child was ill
And gave them juice and pill after pill
Who would gladly have taken their baby's place
Than to see the pain on their little one's face
And the first day of school always came too soon
It felt like we were sending our child to the moon
Then came the games we went to ad infinitum
And, also, the countless goodies we always baked for them
And the planned birthday parties and picnics too
Not to mention the gifts for the entire crew
And then when your child became a teen
You'd worry about where they had been
You'd look up to God and whisper a prayer
And think in your heart and wonder if there
Might not be an easier way
To get your teen through another day
But let's not forget the fathers too
A child needs both to guide them through
Both life's calm waters and stormy seas

So they can grow strong with greater ease
But then comes love all over again
And you prepare for a wedding and then
Little grandchildren, what we have waited for
And it doesn't seem like it's been such a chore
That you've put your whole heart in this marvelous adventure
Because, after all, you were creating a future
And mankind, one day, will thank you so much
For you have given eternity through your touch

BUT WHERE IS THE BABY JESUS?

Chocolate Santas in the candy store
Sugar bells, candy canes and so much more
Snow men in lawns, ten feet tall
Santa and his reindeer arrive at the mall
But where is the Baby Jesus?

There are presents to buy, cards to address
Packages to send that add to the stress
Fudge, divinity all kinds of scrumptious food
The song "White Christmas" to put us in the mood
But where is the Baby Jesus?

Where is the child whose day we celebrate?
Has he met with some terrible fate?
Where have we hidden him, what have we done?
Where have we put God's beloved son?
I know where he'd like to dwell where he'd like to be
In your heart and my heart where the world could see The
Baby Jesus

GENETICS

Do you think we're carrying genetics a bit too far?
I read an article the other day that gave me quite a jar
It stated they are putting firefly genes in the tobacco plant
Does this mean your cigarette will automatically light up if you can't?
And the scientists have created for us a sensation
Another really neat and great innovation
If you do not want the entire cigarette
It will snuff itself out in case you forget
And I just saw, of all things, we are cloning cats
Next time will we clone those creepy old rats?
I was not aware a shortage of cats had been made
In fact, they ask us to have them neutered or spayed
After 87 attempts, they produced only one cat
Nature certainly does much better than that
It frightens me on one hand we are getting so smart
That sometimes we find ourselves in a corner apart
Where we can't figure out what move should be next
Because somebody forgot to write the rest of the text
In Ezra God said, and I'm sure that it's true
Before you were in the womb I had plans for you
If we clone ourselves will anyone win?
Will we have to share our soul like a Siamese twin
Shares their earthly bodies in order to survive?
Or will one have to die for the other to stay alive?
Is this something that has already been done
Eons and eons ago under a much younger sun?

Man may be able to make a clone
But souls are made by God alone
Now a computer chip can be placed under the skin, I am told
It seems things are getting scary and quite bold
If the chip were implanted in us would it be
The last we would see of our cherished privacy?
It will not only tell them who we are but where we have been
With all this info is there anyway a person can win?
I'm told much information can be stored on this chip
Sensitive medical information, secret codes, what a trip
If I forget my name and Alzheimer's overtakes me
Could I have a chip that explains the theory of relativity?
So if friends come to visit me and I don't know their name
I could surprise them with how intelligent I became
We're also cloning everything from loaves to fishes
And adding genes to food to make it more delicious
We can now drink milk from cows that have been cloned
Except by the FDA it has not been condoned
I know it's sometimes hard to gracefully grow old
When parts of our bodies won't do as they're told
And it takes an hour to get out of bed
And feels like our body is made out of lead
But I don't feel that I need to prolong
My life on earth for I feel that it's wrong
When my body falls apart and my eyesight grows dim
To keep replacing all my body parts ad infinitum
Does it help to remember the days of yore
And all the good times that have gone before?
Lord, when I come to the end of my days
Help me to praise thee and count all the ways
You've blest my life while here on this earth
And filled my life with laughter and mirth
Fill the rest of my life with my loving family and friends
That they may remember me with kindness when my life ends.

I LIKE SUMMER BUT……

When summertime comes and bugs fly around
I try to avoid them even though they abound
I do love butterflies though, they give me a thrill
They can light on my hand or wherever they will
But there's an insect that strikes terror in my heart
It's the wasp, that nasty old bug with a dart
It really scares me when it gets in the house
Honestly, I would rather encounter a mouse
They make my skin crawl; I can almost feel their sting
I know you're probably thinking, gosh, what a ding-a-ling
I got one in my house and as you might guess
It was in the bathroom, talk about stress
What should I do? I could call my son
Or I could call my neighbor, no she's 91
I thought this is silly, get hold of yourself
See what kind of spray you have on your shelf
I had no wasp spray but I thought I would try
The ant and roach spray that I saw close by
I grabbed that spray and the fly swatter too
Can't be too armed for the job I must do
I sprayed him hard, didn't faze him a bit
I grabbed the fly swatter, better make a direct hit
It stunned him, he fell in the sink
I turned on the hot water before he could think
I pulled the stopper and flushed him down the drain
I ran it 'til I was sure he was feeling no pain
Then I plugged up the sink to make sure he was dead
There's no point in taking any chances I said

I had another wasp in my house today
But I opened the door and he flew away
I breathed a huge sigh of relief
Why do wasps give me such grief?
I went into the bathroom to powder my face
I turned on the light, got my cosmetic case
'When what to my wondering eyes should appear.'
But another darned wasp, how did he get in here?
So I'm still stuck with the insect I most detest
Please give me a solution so I can get some rest.

.

IN THIS NEW YEAR

In this New Year I wish you peace
And days of joy that never cease

In this New Year may you share the love
The kind God sent us from above

In this New Year may you offer hope
And help that troubled one to cope

And in this New Year may the joy you give
Be what he needs to help him live

In this New Year try to give a smile
And also go that extra mile

And most of all my prayer, you see
In this New Year, please let it be

That we may all with one accord
Follow the teachings of our Lord.

IS THIS WHAT GOD MIGHT SAY?

I am not wanted in school anymore,
My name is not hallowed as it once was before
They don't want My commandments in the courtroom at all
But if My children heard them they might not fall
For if they are never taught right from wrong
Then how will My children ever grow strong.
What kind of hope can their future hold,
If My children have all strayed away from the fold?
The time in this life is not very long
So make sure the path you choose is not wrong.
Are you thankful for the people who fought
And gave their life for the freedom they sought?
Are you thankful for the families who pray
For their safe return each passing day?
You must keep the faith your forefathers started
The world today is not for the fainthearted.
So try to renew your faith every day
And trust in My unchanging way
For I will not leave you if you truly believe
Even though Satan might try to deceive
Stay close to Me, I will always protect
You from Satan and will ever deflect
His arrows of hate that are hurled your way
To keep you safe to My judgment day
My children please know I really do care
I sent My Son your sins to bear.

JUST THINKING

Sometimes I get to thinking about how life began
When God created the Heavens with His almighty hand
Then I try to make connections, I try to make some sense
Of the scientific theories so as not to seem so dense
Are people like the universe that constantly expands?
Whenever we get older must we loosen our waistbands?
The Theory of Uncertainty has left me so perplexed
Can I calculate my kid's speed but not know where he'll be next?
I know that there are black holes or so we have been told
They are stars that lost their glitter and simply got too old
And worm holes seem so exciting, the entrance to another world
I'd like to come out as Marilyn Monroe with my blonde hair permanently curled
And those quasars, ah those quasars, so brilliant and so bright
And scientists when they view them cannot fathom such great light
Their light is of many galaxies colliding in outer space
It is enough to boggle the mind my weak brain can't stand the pace
If I had the brain of Einstein how happy I would be
Minus, of course his hair, that's definitely not for me
Oh, life is so exciting how can anyone be bored?
The changing of the seasons, what beauty they afford
I'll always love to explore the wonders of God's world
And just enjoy the mysteries as they become unfurled

MY THOUGHTS ON CHRISTMAS

My thoughts often wander to Christmases of yore
When we celebrated the birth of the Christ child we adore
When the churches would be packed and the children would perform
The coming of our Savior and people's feelings were so warm
The singing of the carols, they never will grow old
Neither does the story every year when it's retold
And even in school, Christ was allowed to appear
As students remembered His birth every year
But now things have changed and He is no longer welcome
At various places our voices have to stay mum
We have to be so politically correct
And make sure we don't offend any sect
I don't know about you but I feel life is brief
Why must we always give God so much grief?
And this little baby who gave up his life
Why do we give Him such terrible strife?
When I see all the toys and gifts in the store
And Santa appears to offer us more
I remember as a child I enjoyed them too
And I would ask him for lots of toys brand new
But let's not forget what the first Christmas celebrated
And why the angels who sang were so very elated
And who the wise men traveled so far to see
Or why the shepherds worshiped Him on bended knee
So when somebody asks why you celebrate this way
And honor Jesus on Christmas Day
Just look up at them, smile and then say
Hey! Whose birthday is it anyway?

ON GROWING OLD

There are positive things about growing old
When winter comes I can stay in from the cold
I don't have to go to work every day
I can stay in bed or do whatever I may
And if I want to go eat out at noon
I don't have to hurry or leave so soon
But can enjoy the meal and converse with my friend
And remember the rat race I thought wouldn't end
May I help you with groceries, they ask at the store
I love being helped as I walk toward the door
But I wonder if they do this because I look old
Or only because that's what they've been told
And as the hairs on my head keep falling out
Well, that just leaves less hairs for God to count
And frees Him up for more important things
To cure me of the ills that old age brings
I used to be amused at my mother when she
Would first open the paper to the obituary
But now I find myself looking to see
If there are any dead people younger than me
And when I think of all my aches and pains
Arthritis, flabby arms and varicose veins
It tells me I'm going to have to exercise
And cut out all those scrumptious cream pies
I haven't gained that much weight all around
But what I have has shifted terribly toward the ground
Every time my clothes are washed they seem to shrink

They don't make them like they used to I think
And please dear Lord if it be Thy will
Let them find an Alzheimer's pill
For I feel some days I'm headed that way
And could arrive in that state most any day
I had a major senior moment once
Unfortunately it lasted almost six months
I'd attended the 50th reunion of my class
Although we had all aged it was really a gas
My classmates wanted some of the pictures I took
But then I forgot where I had put the book
That had all their names and addresses too
Now what in the world was I going to do?
I looked and I looked and I racked my brain
I thought and I thought 'til my brain was in pain
One day while I was getting my winter clothes out
I rummaged through the mess and let out a shout
Underneath the clothes I took a second look
By golly, there was that little old book
So I had to 'fess up what happened to me
And hope that my classmates would tend to agree
That we all have days we're not at our best
Maybe at our age we just need more rest
But I think back on the years how fast they've gone
Like a fast moving train racing on and on
So I think to myself as I sit down to rest
These golden years are really the best
And I really should spend more time with my friends
So that when my journey on this earth ends
I can leave it behind and say with a smile
That maybe my life was really worthwhile.

PREPOSITIONS

When I called Marilyn about our topic for January I thought she said proposition. Well, that would definitely have to be a fictional story but then she corrected me and said, "No, I said preposition," which didn't help. Any time I can't think of anything to write I always fall back on writing a poem so here goes.

There once was a noun that was really quite bold
He was no ordinary noun I am told
Who felt too important to do only one duty
I guess you could say he was really quite snooty
So one day he approached all the powers that be
You know the ones that make it their job to see
To make sure English is spoken properly
What is it you want little noun they ask?
To be a preposition and perform that task
I want to be a connector and finish the thought
To be more than a noun I have constantly sought
I'm better than that and I know I can do
The task of any preposition too
Well, the powers that be, they all rolled their eyes
And let out such loud and pitiful sighs
Little noun, they asserted, a preposition you can't be
For you must always be a noun can't you see
You cannot be beneath or against but you can be a table
You cannot be beside or on but you can be a label
Don't even ask to be down or despite
These are prepositions and it just isn't right
Throughout, along they don't belong to you
You're a noun but that's no reason to be blue
'Cause you're important just as you are
Without you a sentence would not go far
So please don't be anything but a noun
And don't feel like you should put yourself down
Because we have made it a rule that you
Can't be anything else in this literary zoo.

THE FLAG

I am the flag of your country.
 Many times you have carried me into the fray
My Stars and Stripes have been tattered and torn.
Many men have seen death by the end of the day

In 1777 I was officially born with thirteen stars on a field of
blue
 And thirteen stripes of red and white to represent our colonies
new.

Some say I was at Concord
When the shot was heard 'round the world
And at Lexington too when my colors were unfurled

At Ft. McHenry Francis Scott Key in 1814
Composed a song about me
The words of that song have become our guide
And a beacon by which our people abide

In 1831 I was given another name
Old Glory was also what I became

During World War 1 or the Great War as they state
My stars were increased to forty-eight

And during World War II I rallied our land
With the campaign of United We Stand.

From 1950 to '53 I fought the Korean War
A war we would neither win nor lose
But wind up in an uneasy truce

In 1959 to '75 I fought in Vietnam
I was stepped on and set afire
By people in my country land
And destroyed to show their ire.

We are now engaged in another war
A war for the souls of men
Not one that is of flesh and blood
It is one that condemns our sin

I urge you now to remember me
As I was when my country was born
Or the colors I carry, the red, white and blue
Will once again be tattered and torn.

T'WAS THE DAY BEFORE

T'was the day before housecleaning I lay down to rest
I thought I deserved it so I could give it my best
I looked at the ceiling that I planned to repaint
I was almost asleep my eyesight grew faint
When what through the slits in my eyes should appear
But a battalion of ants in full combat gear
Up from the bed I flew in a flash
And on to the cabinet made a mad dash
All across the ceiling and down on the plants
There marched that mighty parade of ants
What's this in my head that I think that I hear?
It's the ant captain calling his troops from the rear
Now Cedric, now Henry, now Rufus and Paul
And Kerry and Horace now give it your all
Good grief, he's calling his army to war
Well, by golly, this is just going too far
I mounted a chair to get a good shot
Pushed hard on the trigger with all that I got
I hit one and then I saw him fall
I couldn't tell if it was Rufus or Paul
He landed on the floor and got right to his feet
And right away beat a hasty retreat
But instead of heading straight to the door
They ran right across to the kitchen floor
And on to the counter they started to raid
All the food for my lunch that I had just made
But I was determined I would not be defeated
I squirted as I ran and a few were deleted

Some had made it up to my apple pie
And some to my sandwich-smoked ham on rye
The cheese curls were becoming dotted with black
I ran to the cabinet and quick closed the sack
I had squirted so much I was now getting sick
I had to do something and it better be quick
I had heard somewhere it was sugar they craved
So I put some in a line to see how they behaved
At first nothing happened but then they began
To follow the path and ate as they ran
Now Cedric, now Henry, now Rufus and James
I can't believe I'm calling their names
I think I must be getting delirious
'cause I know my problem is quite serious
I drew a sugar line all across the floor
And made sure it went straight up to the door
Like good little soldiers they followed their leader
I had to admire their straight structured meter
They followed the sugar down the porch to the street
The captain looked back as they made their retreat
"Don't worry," he said, "I know what we'll do."
"Next time we'll bring all our relatives too."

WANDERINGS AND WONDRINGS

Sometimes my heart yearns to wander
To my childhood and ponder
The scenes less confusing
Than in this world of bemusing
Lives that are beleaguered
By values that have triggered
Violence and rage
In this crazy age
Where right is sometimes wrong
And hate seems so very strong
Where morals are disappearing
And replaced by acts less endearing
Oh, take me back to those bygone days
And let me embrace those simpler ways
When on Sunday we worshipped the Lord
And believed what was printed in his Holy Word
We could walk anywhere and not have to fear
But now that has all gone with yesteryear
I miss all the family and friends I have lost
But I do feel fortunate that our lives have crossed
They each were very important to me
And all played a part in what I would be
In school we pledged allegiance to the flag
Now some treat it like a dirty old rag
We would say a verse from the Bible each day
And we would even bow our heads and pray
I'm so thankful for the men who have fought
Who died valiantly for the freedom they sought

For the family who prays so that soldiers may
Return to their home safely some day
We must keep the faith our forefathers started
This world today is not for the faint-hearted
So try to renew with each passing day
Your faith in God and his unchanging way.

WHAT DO YOU DO WITH LEFTOVER GRAVY

There are many foods that I like reheated
But there is one that has me completely defeated.
When I make the stuff it just grows and grows,
And what to do with it no one knows.
So maybe you can help me before it gets dumped,
Because I confess, I'm completely stumped.
Oh, what do you do with leftover gravy?
Give it to the U.S. Navy?
Well I tried that- I talked to the guy in command
"Sir", I said sweetly, "I have this gravy on hand."
After a pause, he snickered, "sorry ma'am, that stuff's too thick.
It tends to make our battleships stick
And as you know that can be quite dangerous
Against what the enemy might arrange for us.
So concerning your offer I must decline.
Have you tried the U.S. Mariines-ah, I mean Marines?"
And with that he hung up the phone
And once again I was all alone-with my gravy
Then I thought, gosh, what can I lose
I'll buzz those loyal knights in blue.
I got the captain right away
I said "hello." He said "good day."
I said "Sir" I have this gravy here."
"Hello, hello," clunk! "Ouch, that hurt my ear!
Oh what will I do with this Trojan horse?
I know, I'll call the U.S. Air Force
I started a bit different, I spoke with command
"I have this really secret weapon on hand."

I could hear heavy breathing at the end of the line
I took this to be a favorable sign
"What is it?" he whispered, his voice filled with fear.
"It's gravy, Sir, I said loud and clear,
"You can seed the clouds with it and make it rain
You can drown all the enemy in forest or plain and
You could use the lumps for islands, of course
Oh, I should have told that to the Navy, not the Air Force."
There was total silence at the end of the line
Then I heard a loud thump, that was not a good sign.
So I quickly hung up, I told myself, keep calm, keep cool
I'll pour all this gravy right into our pool
We'll keep it through winter and let it all freeze
We'll use it for an ice rink, that's sure to please.
So if you're in the neighborhood just bring your skates.
It may be a bit lumpy but we have the best rates.

YOU HAVE THE CHOICE

Oh precious little one, soon to be born
Will it be time to rejoice or a time to mourn?
Will your mother choose to let you live
To bless the world with all you can give?
Will she make the choice her mother gave her
Or death for you that she will prefer?
Will she decide that you really don't count
That your life is not worth any amount?
Are you an insignificant part of her life
Something to give her a short time of strife?
Will she decide to end your life that quick
Or let you be born, which one will she pick?
It's up to your mother which road she will take
I pray it's the right one for yours and her sake
I know I won't be there but I'll utter a prayer
To let you know God really does care
You were known long ago by your Father in heaven
But sometimes man takes away what is given
He knew you before you entered the womb
And did not plan it should be your tomb
So precious little, one soon to be born
Will it be a time to rejoice or a time to mourn?

Made in the USA
San Bernardino, CA
19 August 2014